Men of Iron

by HOWARD PYLE

Cover design by Dom Lupo

SCHOLASTIC BOOK SERVICES

Published by Scholastic Book Services, a division
of Scholastic Magazines, Inc., New York, N. Y.

Published by Scholastic Book Services, a division of
Scholastic Magazines, Inc.

5th printing.................June 1968

Printed in the U.S.A.

To my friend and critic

J. HENRY HARPER

is inscribed all that may be of worth

in this volume

INTRODUCTION

THE YEAR 1400 opened with more than usual peacefulness in England. Only a few months before, Richard II—weak, wicked, and treacherous —had been dethroned, and Henry IV declared King in his stead. But it was only a seeming peacefulness, lasting but for a little while; for though King Henry proved himself a just and merciful man—as justice and mercy went with the men of iron of those days—and though he did not care to shed blood needlessly, there were many noble families who had been benefited by King Richard during his reign, and who had lost somewhat of their power and prestige from the coming in of the new King.

Among these were a number of great lords —the Dukes of Albemarle, Surrey, and Exeter, the Marquis of Dorset, the Earl of Gloucester, and others—who had been degraded to their former titles and estates, from which King Richard had lifted them. These and others brewed a secret plot to take King Henry's life. This plot might have succeeded had not one of their own number betrayed them.

Their plan had been to fall upon the King and his adherents, and to massacre them during a great tournament, to be held at Oxford. But Henry did not appear at the lists. Whereupon, knowing that he had been lodging at

1

Windsor with only a few attendants, the conspirators marched thither against him. In the meantime the King had been warned of the plot, so that instead of finding him in the royal castle they discovered through their scouts that he had hurried to London, whence he was even then marching against them at the head of a considerable army. So nothing was left them but flight. Some betook themselves one way, some another. Some sought sanctuary here, some there. But one and another, they were all of them caught and killed.

The Earl of Kent—onetime Duke of Surrey—and the Earl of Salisbury were beheaded in the market place at Cirencester. Lord le Despencer—once the Earl of Gloucester—and Lord Lumley met the same fate at Bristol. The Earl of Huntingdon was taken in the Essex fens, carried to the castle of the Duke of Gloucester, whom he had betrayed to his death in King Richard's time, and was there killed by the castle people. Those few who found friends faithful and bold enough to afford them shelter, dragged those friends down in their own ruin.

Just such a case was that of the father of the boy of this story, the blind Lord Gilbert Reginald Falworth, Baron of Falworth and Easterbridge, who, though having no part in the plot, suffered through it ruin, utter and complete.

He had been a faithful counselor and adviser to King Richard, and perhaps it was this, as much and more than his roundabout connection with the plot, that brought upon him the punishment he suffered.

CHAPTER · 1

MYLES FALWORTH was but eight years of age at that time, and it was only afterward, and when he grew old enough to know more of the ins and outs of the matter, that he could remember by bits and pieces the things that happened: how one evening a knight came clattering into the courtyard upon a horse, red-nostriled and smeared with the sweat and foam of a desperate ride—Sir John Dale, a dear friend of the blind lord.

Even though so young, Myles knew that something very serious had happened to make Sir John so pale and haggard, and he dimly remembered leaning against the knight's iron-covered knees, looking up into his gloomy face, and asking him if he was sick to look so strange. Then those who had been too troubled before to notice him sent him to bed, rebellious at having to go so early.

Myles remembered how the next morning, looking out of a window high up under the eaves, he saw a great troop of horsemen come riding into the courtyard beneath, where a powdering of snow had whitened everything. The leader, a knight in black armor, dismounted and entered the great hall doorway below, followed by several of the band.

He remembered how some of the castle women were standing in a frightened group on the landing of the stairs, talking together in low voices about a matter he did not understand, excepting that the armed men who had ridden into the courtyard had come for Sir John Dale. None of the women paid any attention to him; so he ran off down the winding stairs, expecting every moment to be called back again by one of them.

A crowd of castle people, all very serious and quiet, were gathered in the hall, where a number of strange men-at-arms lounged on the benches, while two billmen in steel caps and leather jackets stood guarding the great door, the butts of their weapons resting on the ground, the staves crossed, barring the door.

In the anteroom was the knight in black armor whom Myles had seen from the window. He was sitting at the table, his great helmet lying on the bench beside him, and a quart beaker of spiced wine at his elbow. A clerk sat at the other end of the same table, with inkhorn in one hand and pen in the other, a parchment spread in front of him.

Master Robert, the castle steward, stood before the knight, who every now and then put to him a question, which the other would answer, and the clerk would write the answer down upon the parchment.

His father stood with his back to the fireplace, looking down on the floor with his blind eyes, his brows drawn moodily together, and the scar of the great wound that he had received at the tournament at York—the wound that had made him blind—showing red across his forehead, as it always did when he was angered or troubled.

There was something about it all that frightened Myles, who crept to his father's side, and slid his little hand into the palm that hung limp and inert. In answer to the touch, his father grasped the hand tightly, but did not seem otherwise to notice that he was there. Neither did the black knight pay any attention to him, but continued questioning Master Robert.

Then, suddenly, there was a commotion in the outer hall—loud voices, and hurrying here and there. The black knight half rose, grasping a heavy iron mace that lay on the bench beside him, and the next moment Sir John Dale himself, as pale as death, walked into the antechamber. He stopped in the very middle of the room. "I yield me to my lord's grace and mercy," said he to the black knight. They were the last words he uttered.

The black knight shouted out some words of command, and swinging up the iron mace in his hand, strode forward, clanking, to Sir John, who raised his arm as though to shield himself from the blow. Two or three of those who stood in the outer hall came running into the room with drawn swords and bills, and little Myles, crying out with terror, hid his face in his father's long gown.

The next instant came the sound of a heavy blow and of a groan, then another blow, and the sound of one falling upon the ground. Then the clashing of steel, and in the midst Lord Falworth crying in a dreadful voice, "Traitor! Coward! Murderer!"

Master Robert snatched Myles away from his father, and bore him out of the room in spite of his screams and struggles. He remembered just one instant's sight of Sir John lying still and silent on his face, and of the black knight standing above him, with the terrible mace in his hand stained a dreadful red.

It was the next day that Lord and Lady Falworth and little Myles, together with three of the more faithful of their people, left the castle.

His memory of past things held a picture for Myles of old Diccon Bowman standing over him in the silence of midnight with a lighted lamp in his hand, and with it a recollection of being bidden to hush when he would have spoken, and of being dressed by Diccon and one of the women, bewildered with sleep, shuddering and chattering with cold.

He remembered being wrapped in the sheepskin that lay at the foot of his bed, and of being carried in Diccon Bowman's arms down the silent darkness of the winding stairway, with the great black giant shadows swaying and flickering upon the wall.

Below were his father and mother and two or three others. A stranger stood warming his hands at a newly made fire, and little Myles, as he peeped from out the warm sheepskin, saw that he was in riding boots and was covered with mud. He did not know until long years afterward that the stranger was a messenger sent by a friend at the King's court, bidding his father fly for safety.

Then Diccon Bowman carried him out into the strangeness of the winter midnight.

Outside, beyond the frozen moat, where the reeds stood stark and stiff in their winter nakedness, was a group of dark figures waiting for them with horses. In the pallid moonlight Myles recognized Father Edward, the Prior of St. Mary's.

After that came a long ride through that silent night upon the saddlebow in front of Diccon Bowman; then a deep, heavy sleep, fell upon him in spite of the galloping of the horses.

When next he awoke the sun was shining, and his home and his whole life were changed.

CHAPTER · 2

FROM THE TIME the family escaped from Falworth Castle that midwinter night to the time Myles was sixteen he knew nothing of the great world beyond Crosbey-Dale. A fair was held twice in a twelvemonth at the market town of Wisebey, and three times in the seven years, old Diccon Bowman took the lad to see the sights at that place. Beyond these three glimpses of the outer world he lived almost as secluded a life as one of the monks of St. Mary's Priory.

Crosbey-Dale, their new home, was different enough from Falworth or Easterbridge Castle, the former baronial seats of Lord Falworth. It was a long, low, straw-thatched farmhouse. Once, when the church lands were divided into two holdings, it was one of the bailiff's houses. All around were the fruitful farms of the Priory, tilled by well-to-do tenant holders, and rich with fields of waving grain and meadowlands. In those days the church lands were under church rule, and were governed by church laws, and there, when war and famine blighted the outside world, harvests flourished. The Prior of St. Mary's owed much if not all of the church's prosperity to the blind Lord Falworth, and now he was paying it back with a haven of refuge for his former patron.

I wonder what boys today would have thought of Myles' training. With him that training was not only of the mind, but of the body as well, and for seven years it was almost unremitting. "Ye have your own way to make in the world," his father said more than once when the boy complained of the grinding hardness of his life, and to make one's way in those days meant a thousand times more than it does now. It meant not only a heart to feel and a brain to think, but a hand quick and strong to strike in battle, and a body tough to endure the wounds and blows in return. And so it was that Myles' body as well as his mind had to be trained to meet the needs of the dark age in which he lived.

Every morning, winter or summer, rain or shine, he tramped away six long miles to the Priory school, and in the evenings his mother taught him French.

"Why must I learn that vile tongue?" asked he.

"Call it not vile," said the blind old lord grimly. "When ye are grown a man ye'll have to seek your fortune in France, for England is no place for those of Falworth blood." And in afteryears, true to prediction, the "vile tongue" served him well.

As for his physical training, that pretty well filled up the hours between his morning studies at the monastery and his evening studies at home. Then it was that old Diccon Bowman took him in hand. The old bowman had served with Lord Falworth's father under the Black Prince, both in France and Spain, and in long years of war had gained a practical knowledge of arms that few could surpass. Besides the use of the broadsword, the short sword, the quarterstaff, and the cudgel, he taught Myles to shoot so skillfully with the longbow and the crossbow that not a lad in the countryside was his match at the village butts. Attack and defense with the lance and throwing the knife and dagger were also part of his training.

Then, in addition to this more regular part of his physical training, Myles was taught in another branch not so often included in the military education of the day—the art of wrestling. It happened that a fellow lived in Crosbey village, by name Ralph-the-Smith, who was the greatest wrestler in the countryside, and had worn the champion belt for three years. Every Sunday afternoon, in fair weather, he came to teach Myles the art; and being wonderfully adept in bodily feats, Myles soon could cast any lad under twenty.

"It is an ungentle armscraft that he learns," said Lord Falworth one day to Prior Edward. "Except for the broadsword, the dagger, and the lance, there is but little that a gentleman of his birth may use. Nevertheless, he gains quickness and suppleness, and if he has true blood in his veins he will acquire knightly arts shrewdly quick when the time comes to learn them."

But hard and grinding as Myles' life was, it was not entirely without pleasures. There were many boys living in Crosbey-Dale and the village; yeomen's and farmers' sons, to be sure, but nevertheless lads of his own age, and that, after all, is the main requirement for friendship in boyhood's world. Then there was the river to bathe in. There were the hills and valleys to roam over.

Once he gained a triumph that for many a day was very sweet. As was said before, he had been three times to the market town at fair time, and on the last of these occasions he had fought a bout of quarterstaff with a young fellow of twenty, and had been the conqueror. He was fourteen.

Old Diccon, who had gone with him to the fair, had met some cronies of his own, with whom he had sat gossiping in the ale booth, leaving Myles to shift for himself. By and by the old man had noticed a crowd gathered at one part of the fairground, and, sensing a fight, had gone running, ale pot in hand. Then, peering over the shoulders of the crowd, he had seen his young master, stripped to the waist, fighting like a gladiator with a fellow a head taller than himself. Diccon was about to force his way through the crowd and drag them asunder, but a second look had showed his practiced eye that Myles was not only holding his own, but was in the way of winning the victory. So he stood with the others looking on, withholding himself from any interference and whatever upbraiding might be necessary until the fight had been brought to a triumphant close. Lord Falworth never heard directly of the redoubtable affair, but old Diccon was not so silent with the common folk of Crosbey-Dale, and so no doubt the father had some inkling of what had happened.

It was shortly after this notable event that Myles was formally initiated into squirehood. His father and mother, as was the custom, stood sponsors for him. By them, each bearing a lighted taper, he was escorted to the altar. It was at St. Mary's Priory, and Prior Edward blessed the sword and girded it to the lad's side. No one was present but the four, and when the good Prior had given the benediction and had signed the cross upon his forehead, Myles' mother stooped and kissed his brow. Henceforth Myles had the right to wear a sword.

Myles had ended his fifteenth year. He had a bonny brown face, curling hair, a square, strong chin, and a pair of merry, laughing blue eyes; his shoulders were broad; his chest was thick of girth; his muscles were tough as oak.

The day upon which he was sixteen, as he came whistling home from the monastery school, he was met by Diccon Bowman.

"Master Myles," said the old man, with a snuffle in his voice—"Master Myles, your father would see you in his chamber, and bade me send you to him as soon as ye did come home. Oh, Master Myles, I fear me ye are going to leave home."

Myles stopped short. "Leave home!" he cried.

"Aye," said old Diccon, "ye may go to some grand castle to live, and be a page there, and then a gentleman-at-arms in some great lord's pay."

"What is this about castles and lords and gentlemen-at-arms?" said Myles. "Are ye jesting?"

"Nay," said Diccon, "I am not jesting. But go to your father, and then ye will presently know all. Only I do say it is likely ye leave us tomorrow."

And so it was as Diccon had said. Myles was to leave home the very next morning. He found his father and mother and Prior Edward waiting.

"We three have been talking it over this morning," said his father, "and think that the time has come for you to quit this poor home of ours. If ye stay here ten years longer, ye will be no more fit to go then than now. Tomorrow I will give you a letter to my kinsman, the Earl of Mackworth. He has thrived in these days and I have fallen, but time was that he and I

were true sworn companions, and plighted together in friendship never to be sundered. I
think, as I remember him, he will abide by his
plighted troth, and will give you his aid to rise
in the world. So, as I said, tomorrow morning
ye shall set forth with Diccon Bowman, and
shall go to Castle Devlen, and there deliver this
letter, which prays him to give you a place in
his household. Ye may have this afternoon to
yourself to make ready such things as ye shall
take with you. And send Diccon to me. He
must take the gray horse to the village and
have it shod."

Prior Edward had been standing looking out
of the window. As Lord Falworth ended, he
turned.

"And, Myles," said he, "ye will need some
money, so I will give you as a loan forty shillings, which someday ye may return to me. For
know this, Myles, a man cannot do in the world
without money. Your father has it ready for
you in the chest, and will give it you tomorrow before ye go."

The next morning Myles, with the old bowman, rode out into the great world to seek his
fortune.

CHAPTER · 3

WHAT MYLES REMEMBERED of Falworth loomed
great and grand and big, as things do in the
memory of childhood, but even memory could

not make Falworth the equal of Devlen Castle, when, as he and Diccon Bowman rode out of Devlen town across the great rude stone bridge that spanned the river, he first saw, rising above the crowns of the trees, those huge hoary walls and the steep roofs and chimneys clustered together, like the roofs and chimneys of a town.

The castle was built upon a plateaulike rise of ground, which was enclosed by the outer wall. It was surrounded on three sides by a looplike bend of the river, and on the fourth was protected by a deep, broad, artificial moat, almost as wide as the stream from which it was fed. The road from the town wound for a little distance along by the edge of this moat. As Myles and the old bowman galloped by, with the answering echo of their horses' hoofbeats rattling back from the smooth stone face of the walls, the lad looked up, wondering at the height and strength of the great ancient fortress. In his air-castle building Myles had pictured the Earl receiving him as the son of his onetime comrade in arms—receiving him, perhaps, with somewhat of the rustic warmth that he knew at Crosbey-Dale. But now, as he stared at those massive walls from below, and realized his own insignificance and the greatness of this Earl, he felt the first keen, helpless ache of homesickness shoot through his breast, and his heart yearned for Crosbey-Dale again.

Then they thundered across the bridge that spanned the moat, and through the dark shadows of the great gaping gateway, and Diccon, bidding him stay for a moment, rode forward to speak to the gatekeeper.

The gatekeeper gave the two in charge of one of the men-at-arms who were lounging upon a bench in the archway, who in turn gave them into the care of one of the house servants in the outer courtyard. So, having been passed from one to another, and having answered many questions, Myles finally found himself in the outer waiting room sitting beside Diccon upon a wooden bench that stood along the wall under the great arch of a glazed window.

For a while the poor country lad sat stupidly bewildered. He was aware of people coming and going. He was aware of talk and laughter sounding around him, but he thought of nothing but his aching homesickness and the oppression of his utter littleness in the busy life of this great castle.

Meantime old Diccon Bowman was staring about him with huge interest, every now and then nudging his young master, calling his attention now to this and now to that, until at last the lad began to awaken somewhat from his despondency to the things around. Besides those servants and others who came and went, and a knot of six or eight men-at-arms with bills and poleaxes who stood at the farther doorway talking together in low tones, now and then broken by a stifled laugh, was a group of four young squires who lounged on a bench beside a doorway hidden by a curtain, and upon them Myles' eyes lit with a sudden interest. Three of the four were about his own age, one was a year or two older, and all four were dressed in the black-and-yellow uniform of the house of Beaumont.

Myles plucked the bowman by the sleeve. "Are they squires, Diccon?" said he, nodding toward the door.

"Eh?" said Diccon. "Aye; they're squires."

"And will my station be with them?" asked the boy.

"Aye; if the Earl takes you to service, ye will haply be taken as squire."

Myles stared at them, and then of a sudden was aware that the young men were talking of him. He knew it by the way they eyed him and spoke now and then in one another's ears. One of the four, a gay young fellow, with long riding boots laced with green laces, said a few words, the others gave a laugh, and poor Myles, knowing how ungainly he must seem to them, felt the blood rush to his cheeks, and shyly turned his head.

Suddenly, as though stirred by an impulse, the same lad who had just created the laugh arose from the bench and came directly across the room to where Myles and the bowman sat.

"Give ye good day," said he. "What is your name and whence come ye, if I may make so bold to ask?"

"My name is Myles Falworth," said Myles; "and I come from Crosbey-Dale bearing a letter to my lord."

"Never did I hear of Crosbey-Dale," said the squire. "But what seek ye here, if I may ask that much?"

"I come seeking service," said Myles, "and would enter as an esquire such as ye be in my lord's household."

Myles' new acquaintance grinned. "Ye'll make

a droll squire to wait in a lord's household," said he. "Have ye ever been in such service?"

"Nay," said Myles. "I have only been at school, and learned Latin and French and what not. But Diccon Bowman here has taught me use of arms."

The young squire laughed outright. "By Our Lady, your talk tickles me, friend Myles," said he. "Think ye such matters will gain you footing here? But stay! Ye did say that ye had a letter to my lord. From whom is it?"

"It is from my father," said Myles. "He is of noble blood, but fallen in estate. He is a kinsman of my lord, his onetime comrade-in-arms."

"So?" said the other. "Then perhaps your chances are not so ill after all." Then, after a moment, he added: "My name is Francis Gascoyne, and I will stand your friend in this matter. Get your letter ready, for my lord and his Grace of York are within, and come forth soon. The Archbishop is on his way to Dalworth, and my lord escorts him as far as Uppingham. I and those others are to go along. Do ye know my lord by sight?"

"Nay," said Myles, "I know him not."

"Then I will tell you when he comes. Listen!" said he, as a confused clattering sounded in the outer courtyard. "Yonder are the horses now. They come presently. Better have your letter ready, friend Myles."

The attendants who passed through the anteroom now came and went more hurriedly, and Myles knew that the Earl must be about to come forth. He had hardly time to untie his pouch, take out the letter, and tie the strings again when the curtain at the doorway was thrust suddenly aside, and a tall, thin squire of about twenty came forth, said some words to the young men on the bench, and then withdrew again. Instantly the squires arose and took their station beside the doorway. A sudden hush fell upon all in the room, and the men-at-arms stood in a line against the wall, stiff and erect as though all at once transformed to figures of iron. Once more the curtain was drawn back, and in the hush Myles heard voices in the other room.

"My lord comes," whispered Gascoyne in his ear, and Myles felt his heart leap in answer.

The next moment two noblemen came into the anteroom, followed by a crowd of gentlemen, squires, and pages. One of the two was a dignitary of the Church. The other Myles instantly singled out as the Earl of Mackworth.

CHAPTER · 4

HE WAS A TALL MAN, taller even than Myles' father. He had a thin face, deep-set bushy eyebrows, and a hawk nose. His upper lip was clean-shaven, but from his chin a flowing beard of iron gray hung nearly to his waist. He was clad in a riding gown of black velvet that hung a little lower than the knee, trimmed with otter fur and embroidered with silver goshawks—the crest of the family of Beaumont.

A light shirt of link mail showed beneath the

gown as he walked, and a pair of soft un-
dressed leather riding boots were laced as high
as the knee, protecting his scarlet hose from
mud and dirt. Over his shoulders he wore a collar of enameled gold from which hung a magnificent jeweled pendant, and upon his fist he
carried a beautiful Iceland falcon.

As Myles stood staring, he suddenly heard
Gascoyne's voice whisper in his ear, "Yonder is
my lord. Go forward and give him your letter."

Scarcely knowing what he did, he walked toward the Earl like a machine, his heart pound-
ing within him and a great humming in his
ears. As he drew near, the nobleman stopped
for a moment and stared at him, and Myles, as
in a dream, kneeled and presented the letter.
The Earl took it in his hand, turned it this way
and that, looked first at the bearer, then at the
packet, and then at the bearer again.

"Who are ye?" he said; "and what is the
matter ye would have of me?"

"I am Myles Falworth," said the lad, in a
low voice, "and I come seeking service with
you."

The Earl drew his thick eyebrows quickly together and shot a keen look at the lad. "Falworth?" said he, sharply—"Falworth? I know no
Falworth!"

"The letter will tell you," said Myles. "It is
from one once dear to you."

"The Earl handed the letter to a gentleman
who stood near, and bade him break the seal.
"Ye may stand," said he to Myles. "Ye need not
kneel there forever." Then, taking the opened
parchment again, he glanced first at the face

and then at the back, and, seeing its length, looked vexed. Then he read for an earnest moment or two, skipping from line to line. Presently he folded the letter and thrust it into the pouch at his side. "So it is, your Grace," said he to the lordly prelate, "that we who have luck to rise in the world must ever suffer by being plagued at all times and seasons. Here is one I chanced to know a dozen years ago, who thinks he has a claim upon me, and saddles me with his son. I must take the lad, too, for the sake of peace and quietness." He glanced around, and seeing Gascoyne, who had drawn near, beckoned to him. "Take this fellow," said he, "to the buttery, and see him fed. And then to Sir James Lee, and have his name entered in the castle books. And stay, sirrah," he added; "bid Sir James, if it may be so done, to enter him as a squire-at-arms. I think he will be better serving so than in the household, for he appears to be a rough cub for a page."

Myles did look rustic enough, standing clad in frieze in the midst of that gay company, and a murmur of laughter sounded around, though he was too bewildered fully to understand that he was the cause of the merriment. Then some hand drew him back—it was Gascoyne's—there was a bustle of people passing, and the next minute they were gone, and Myles and old Diccon Bowman and the young squire were left alone in the anteroom.

Gascoyne looked very sour and put out. "Murrain upon it!" said he. "Here is good sport spoiled for me to see you fed. I wish no ill to you, friend, but I would ye had come this afternoon or tomorrow."

"I bring trouble and dole to everyone," said Myles, somewhat bitterly. "It would have been better had I never come to this place."

His words and tone softened Gascoyne a little. "Never mind," said the squire; "it was not your fault, and is past mending now. So come and fill your stomach, in heaven's name."

Perhaps not the least hard part of the whole trying day for Myles was his parting with Diccon. Gascoyne and he had accompanied the old retainer to the outer gate, in the archway of which they now stood, for without a permit they could go no farther. The old bowman led by the bridle rein the horse upon which Myles had ridden that morning. His own nag, a vicious brute, was restive to be gone, but Diccon held him in with tight rein. He reached down and took Myles' sturdy brown hand in his crooked, knotted grasp.

"Farewell, young master," he croaked, tremulously, with a watery glimmer in his pale eyes. "Ye will not forget me when I am gone?"

"Nay," said Myles; "I will not forget you."

"Aye, aye," said the old man, looking down at him, and shaking his head slowly from side to side; "ye are a great, tall, sturdy fellow now, yet have I held you on my knee many and many's the time, and dandled you when ye were only a little babe. Be still, ye devil's limb!" He suddenly broke off, reining back his restive rawboned steed, which again began to caper and prance. Myles was not sorry for the interruption. He felt awkward and abashed at the parting and at the old man's reminiscences, knowing that Gascoyne's eyes were resting amusedly upon the scene, and that the men-at-arms were looking on. Certainly old Diccon did look droll as he struggled vainly with his vicious, high-necked nag. "Nay, a murrain on you! Ye will go, go!" cried he at last, with a savage dig of his heels into the animal's ribs, and away they clattered, the led horse kicking up its heels as a final parting, setting Gascoyne laughing. At the bend of the road the old man turned and nodded his head. The next moment he had disappeared around the angle of the wall, and it seemed to Myles, as he stood looking after him, as though the last thread that bound him to his old life had snapped and broken. As he turned he saw that Gascoyne was looking at him.

"Do you feel downhearted?" said the young squire, curiously.

"Nay," said Myles, brusquely. Nevertheless, his throat was tight and dry, and the word came huskily in spite of himself.

CHAPTER · 5

THE EARL OF MACKWORTH, as was customary among the great lords in those days, maintained a small army of knights, gentlemen, men-at-arms, and retainers, who were expected to serve him upon all occasions of need, and from whom was supplied his quota of recruits to fill such levies as might be made upon him by the King in time of war.

The knights and gentlemen of this little army of horse and foot soldiers were largely recruited from the company of squires and bachelors, as the young novitiate soldiers of the castle were called.

This company of esquires consisted of from eighty to ninety lads, ranging in age from eight to twenty years. Those under fourteen years were termed pages, and served chiefly the Countess and her waiting gentlewomen, in whose company they acquired the graces and polish of the times, such as they were. After reaching the age of fourteen the lads were allowed to use title of esquire or squire.

In most of the great houses of the time the esquires were the special attendants upon the lord and lady of the house, holding such positions as body squires, cupbearers, carvers, and sometimes the office of chamberlain. But Devlen, like some other of the princely castles of the greatest nobles, was more like a military post or a fortress than an ordinary household. Only comparatively few of the esquires could be used in personal attendance upon the Earl. The others were trained more strictly in arms, and served rather in the capacity of a sort of bodyguard than as ordinary squires. For, as the Earl rose in power and influence, and as it became so well worth while for the lower nobility and gentry to enter their sons in his family, the body of squires became almost cumbersomely large. Accordingly, that part which comprised the squires proper, as separate from the younger pages, was divided into three classes—first, squires of the body, who were those just past pagehood, and who waited upon the Earl in personal service; second, squires of the household, who, having regular hours assigned for exercise in the manual of arms, were relieved from personal service excepting upon special occasions; and third and last, at the head of the whole body of lads, a class called bachelors—young men ranging from eighteen to twenty years of age. This class was supposed to exercise a sort of government over the other and younger squires—to keep them in order as much as possible, to marshal them upon occasions of importance, to see that their arms and equipment were kept in good order, to call the roll for chapel in the morning, and to see that those not on duty in the house were present at the daily exercise at arms. Orders to the squires were generally transmitted through the bachelors, and the head of that body was expected to make weekly reports of affairs in their quarters to the chief captain of the body.

From this overlordship of the bachelors there had gradually risen a system of fagging, such as is or was practiced in the great English public schools—enforced services exacted from the younger lads—which at the time Myles came to Devlen had, in the five or six years it had been in practice, grown to be an absolute though unwritten law of the body—a law supported by all the prestige of long-continued usage. At that time the bachelors numbered but thirteen, yet they exercised over the rest of the sixty-four squires and pages a rule of iron, and were taskmasters, hard, exacting, and oftentimes cruel.

The whole company of squires and pages was under the supreme command of a certain one-eyed knight, by name Sir James Lee, a soldier seasoned by the fire of a dozen battles, bearing a score of wounds won in fight and tourney, and withered by hardship and labor to a leatherlike toughness. He had fought upon the King's side in all the late wars, and had at Shrewsbury received a wound that unfitted him for active service, so that now he was fallen to the post of Captain of Esquires at Devlen Castle—a man disappointed in life, and with a temper embittered by that failure as well as by cankering pain.

Yet perhaps no one could have been better fitted for the place he held than Sir James Lee. The lads under his charge were a rude, rough, unruly set, quick, like their elders, to quarrel, and to quarrel fiercely, even to the drawing of sword or dagger. But there was a cold, iron sternness about the grim old man that quelled them, as the trainer with a lash of steel might quell a den of young wolves. The apartments in which he was lodged with his clerk were next to the dormitory of the lads, and even in the midst of the most excited brawlings the distant sound of his harsh voice, "Silence, messieurs!" would bring an instant hush to the loudest uproar.

It was into his grim presence that Myles was introduced by Gascoyne. Sir James was in his office, a room bare of ornament or adornment or superfluous comfort of any sort—without even so much as a mat of rushes upon the cold stone floor to make it less cheerless. The old one-eyed knight sat gnawing his bristling mustaches. To anyone who knew him it would have been apparent that, as the castle phrase went, "the devil sat astride of his neck," which meant that one of his blind wounds was aching more sorely than usual.

His clerk sat beside him, with account books and parchment spread upon the table, and the head squire, Walter Blunt, a lad some three or four years older than Myles, and half a head taller, black-browed, powerfully built, and with cheek and chin darkened by the soft budding of his adolescent beard, stood making his report.

Sir James listened in grim silence while Gascoyne told his errand.

"So then, pardee, I am bid to take another one of ye, am I?" he snarled. "As though ye caused me not trouble enough. And this one a cub, looking a very boor in carriage and breeding. Maybe the Earl thinks I am to train boys to his dilly-dally household service as well as to use of arms."

"Sir," said Gascoyne, timidly, "my lord says he would have this one entered direct as a squire of the body, so that he need not serve in the household."

"Say ye so?" cried Sir James, harshly. "Then take my message back again to your lord. Not for Mackworth—no, nor a better man than he— will I make any changes in my government. If I be set to rule a pack of boys, I will rule them as I decide, and not according to any man's bidding. Tell him, sirrah, that I will enter no lad as squire of the body without first testing whether he be fit at arms to hold that place." He sat for a while glowering at Myles and gnawing his mustaches, and for the time no one dared to break the grim silence. "What is your name?" said he, suddenly. And then, almost before Myles could answer, he asked the head squire whether he could find a place to lodge him.

"There is Gillis Whitlock's cot empty," said Blunt. "He is in the infirmary, and no doubt goes home again when he comes thence. The fever has gotten into his bones, and—"

"That will do," said the knight, interrupting him impatiently. "Let him take that place, or any other that ye have. And ye, Jerome," said he to his clerk, "ye may enter him upon the roll, though whether it be as page or squire or bachelor shall be as I please, and not as Mackworth bids me. Now get ye gone."

"Old Bruin's wound smarts him sore," Gascoyne observed, as the two lads walked across the armory court. He had good-naturedly offered to show the newcomer the many sights of interest around the castle, and in the hour or so of ramble that followed the two grew from acquaintances to friends with a quickness that boyhood alone can bring about. They visited the armory, the chapel, the stables, the great hall, the Painted Chamber, the guardhouse, the messroom, and even the scullery and the kitchen with its great range of boilers and furnaces and ovens. Last of all Myles' new friend introduced him to the armor smithy.

"My lord has sent a piece of Milan armor here to be repaired," said he. "Would ye like to see it?"

"Aye," said Myles, eagerly, "that would I."

The smith was a gruff, good-natured fellow, and showed the piece of armor to Myles readily and willingly enough. It was a beautiful basinet of inlaid workmanship edged with a rim of gold. Myles scarcely dared touch it. He gazed at it with an unconcealed delight that warmed the smith's honest heart.

"I have another piece of Milan here," said he. "Did I ever show you my dagger, Master Gascoyne?"

"Nay," said the squire.

The smith unlocked a great oaken chest in the corner of the shop, lifted the lid, and brought out a handsome dagger with a handle of ebony and silver gilt and a sheath of Spanish leather, embossed and gilt. The keen, well-tempered blade was beautifully engraved and inlaid with niello work, representing a group of figures in a then popular subject—that dance of Death. It was a weapon at once unique and beautiful, and even Gascoyne showed an admiration scarcely less keen than Myles' openly expressed delight.

"To whom does it belong?" said he, trying the point upon his thumbnail.

"There," said the smith, "is the jest of the whole, for it belongs to me. Sir William Beauclerk bade me order the weapon through Master Gildersworthy of London town, and by the time it came hither, lo! he had died, and so it fell to my hands. No one here pays the price for the trinket, and so I must keep it myself, though I be but a poor man."

"How much do ye hold it for?" Gascoyne.

"Seventeen shillings buys it," said the armorer, carelessly.

"Aye, aye," said Gascoyne, with a sigh; "so it is to be poor and not be able to have such things as one loves and would fain possess. Seventeen shillings is nearly as much by half again as all my yearly wage."

Then a sudden thought came to Myles, and as it came his cheeks glowed as hot as fire. "Master Gascoyne," said he, with gruff awkwardness. "Ye've been a very good, true friend to me since I have come to this place, and have befriended me in all ways ye could, and I, as well I know, but a poor rustic clod. Now I have forty shillings by me which I may spend as I wish, and so I do beseech you to take yon dagger of me as a gift, and have and hold it for your very own."

Gascoyne stared open-mouthed at Myles. "D'ye mean it?" said he, at last.

"Aye," said Myles, "I do mean it. Master Smith, give him the blade."

At first the smith grinned, thinking it all a jest. But he soon saw that Myles was serious enough, and when the seventeen shillings were produced and counted down upon the anvil, he took off his cap and made Myles a low bow as he swept them into his pouch. "Now, by my faith and troth," said he, "that I do call a true lordly gift. Is it not so, Master Gascoyne?"

"Aye," said Gascoyne, with a gulp, "it is in truth."

And thereupon, to Myles' great wonderment, he suddenly flung his arms about his neck, and, giving him a great hug, kissed him on the cheek.

"Dear Myles," said he, "I tell you truly and of a verity I did feel warm toward you from the very first time I saw you sitting like a poor oaf upon the bench up yonder in the anteroom, and now truly I give you assurance that I do love you as my own brother. Yea, I will take the dagger, and will stand by you as a true friend from this time forth. Ye may need a true friend in this place before ye live long with us, for some of us esquires are rough, and knocks are more plenty here than broad pennies, so that one newcome is like to have a hard time gaining a footing."

"I thank you," said Myles, "for your offer of love and friendship, and to tell you, upon my part, that I also of all the world would like best to have you for my friend."

Such was the manner in which Myles formed the first great friendship of his life, a friendship that was destined to last him through many years to come. As the two walked back across the great quadrangle, upon which fronted the main buildings of the castle, their arms were wound across each other's shoulders.

CHAPTER · 6

A BOY'S LIFE is of a very flexible sort. It takes but a little while for it to shape itself to any new surroundings in which it may be thrown, to make itself new friends, to settle itself to new habits. And so it was that Myles fell directly into the ways of the lads of Devlen. On his first morning, as he washed his face and hands with the other squires and pages in a great tank of water in the armory courtyard, he presently found himself splashing and dashing with the others, laughing and shouting as loud as any, and calling some by their Christian names as though he had known them for years instead of overnight. During chapel he watched with sympathetic delight the covert pranks of the youngsters during the half-hour that Father Emmanuel droned his

Latin, and with his dagger point he carved his own name among the many cut deep into the back of the bench before him. When, after breakfast, the squires poured like schoolboys into the great armory to answer to the roll call for daily exercises, he came storming in with the rest, beating the lad in front of him with his cap.

Boys are very keen to feel the influence of a forceful character. A lad with a strong will is quick to reach his proper level as a greater or lesser leader among the others, and Myles was of just the masterful nature to make his individuality felt among the Devlen squires. He was quick enough to yield obedience upon all occasions to proper authority, but would never bend an inch to the usurpation of tyranny. In the school at St. Mary's Priory at Crosbey-Dale he would submit without a murmur or offer of resistance to chastisement by old Father Ambrose, the regular teacher. But once, when the fat old monk was sick, and a great, long-legged, strapping young friar, who had temporarily taken his place, undertook to administer punishment, Myles, with a wrestling trip, flung him sprawling backward over a bench into the midst of a shoal of small boys amid a hubbub of riotous confusion. He had been flogged soundly for it under the supervision of Prior Edward himself. But as soon as his punishment was over, he assured the Prior very seriously that should like occasion again happen he would act in the same manner, flogging or no flogging.

It was this bold, outspoken spirit that gained him at once friends and enemies at Devlen, and though it first showed itself in what was but a little matter, nevertheless it set a mark upon him that singled him out from the rest, and, although he did not suspect it at the time, called him to the attention of Sir James Lee himself, who regarded him as a lad of free and frank spirit.

The first morning after the roll call in the armory, as Walter Blunt, the head bachelor, rolled up the slip of parchment, and the temporary silence burst forth into redoubled noise and confusion, each lad arming himself from a row of racks that stood along the wall, he beckoned Myles to him.

"My lord himself has spoken to Sir James Lee concerning you," said he. "Sir James maintains that he will not enter you into the body until ye have first practiced for a while at the pels, and shown what ye can do at broadsword. Have ye ever fought at the pel?"

"Aye," answered Myles, "and that every day of my life since I became esquire four years ago, saving only Sundays and holy days."

"With shield and broadsword?"

"Sometimes," said Myles, "and sometimes with the short sword."

"Sir James would have you come to the tilt-yard this morning. He himself will take you in hand to see what you can do. Ye may take the arms upon yonder rack and use them until otherwise bidden. Ye sees that the number painted above it on the wall is seventeen. That will be your number for the nonce."

So Myles armed himself from his rack as the others were doing from theirs. The armor was rude and heavy, used to accustom the body to the weight of iron plates rather than for any defense. It consisted of a cuirass, or breastplate of iron, opening at the side with hinges and latching with hooks and eyes; *épaulières*, or shoulder plates; armplates and legpieces; and a basinet, or openfaced helmet. A great triangular shield, covered with leather and studded with bosses of iron, and a heavy broadsword, pointed and dulled at the edges, completed the equipment.

The practice of the pels which Myles was bidden to attend comprised the chief exercise of the day with the esquires of young cadet soldiers of that time, and in it they learned not only all the strokes, cuts, and thrusts of swordplay then in vogue, but also toughness, endurance, and elastic quickness. The pels themselves consisted of upright posts of ash or oak, about five feet six inches in height, and in girth somewhat thicker than a man's thigh. They were firmly planted in the ground, and upon them the strokes of the broadsword were directed.

At Devlen the pels stood just back of the open and covered tilting courts and the archery ranges, and thither those lads not upon household duty were marched every morning except Fridays and Sundays, and were there exercised under the direction of Sir James Lee and two assistants. The whole company was divided into two, sometimes into three parties, each of which took its turn at the exercise, delivering at the word of command the various strokes, feints, attacks, and retreats as the instructors ordered. After five minutes of this mock battle the perspiration began to pour down their faces, and the breath to come thick and short. But it was not until the lads could absolutely endure no more that the order was given to rest, and they were allowed to fling themselves panting upon the ground, while another company took its place at the triple row of posts.

As Myles struck and hacked at the pel assigned to him, Sir James Lee stood beside him watching him in grim silence. The lad did his best to show the knight all that he knew of uppercut, undercut, thrust, and backhand stroke, but it did not seem to him that Sir James was very well satisfied with his skill.

"Ye fight like a clodpole," said the old man. "Ha, that stroke was but ill recovered. Strike me it again, and get ye in guard more quickly."

Myles repeated the stroke.

"Pest!" cried Sir James. "Ye are too slow by a week. Here, strike ye the blow at me."

Myles hesitated. Sir James held a stout staff in his hand, but otherwise he was unarmed.

"Strike, I say!" said Sir James. "What stays ye? Are ye afraid?"

It was Myles' answer that set the seal of individuality upon him. "Nay," said he, boldly, "I am not afraid. I fear not you nor any man!" So saying, he delivered the stroke at Sir James with might and main. It was met with a jarring blow that made his wrist and arm tingle, and the next instant he received a stroke upon the basinet that caused his ears to ring and the sparks to dance and fly before his eyes.

"Pardee!" said Sir James, grimly. "If I had had a mace in my hand, I would have knocked your cockerel brains out that time. Ye may take that blow for answering me so pertly. And now we are quits. Now strike me the stroke again if ye are not afraid."

Myles' eyes watered in spite of himself, and he shut the lids tight to wink the dimness away. Nevertheless he spoke up undauntedly as before. "Aye, marry, will I strike it again," said he. And this time he was able to recover guard quickly enough to turn Sir James' blow with his shield, instead of receiving it upon his head.

"So!" said Sir James. "Now mind you of this, that when ye strike that lower cut at the legs, recover yourself more quickly. Now then, strike at the pel."

Gascoyne and other of the lads who were just then lying stretched out upon the grass beneath a tree at the edge of the open court where stood the pels were interested spectators of the whole scene. Not one of them in their memory had heard Sir James so answered face to face as Myles had answered him, and, after all, perhaps the lad himself would not have done so had he been longer a resident in the squires' quarters at Devlen.

"By Our Lady! ye are a cool blade, Myles," said Gascoyne as they marched back to the armory again. "Never heard I one speak to Sir James as ye have done this day."

"And, after all," said another of the young squires, "old Bruin was not so ill-pleased, I think. That was a shrewd blow he fetched you on the crown, Falworth. Marry, I would not have had it on my own skull for a silver penny."

CHAPTER · 7

So LITTLE DOES IT TAKE to make a body's reputation.

That night all the squires' quarters buzzed with the story of how the new boy, Falworth, had answered Sir James Lee to his face without fear, and had exchanged blows with him hand to hand. Walter Blunt himself was moved to some show of interest.

"What said he to you, Falworth?" asked he.

"He said naught," said Myles, brusquely. "He only sought to show me how to recover from the undercut."

"It is passing strange that he should take so much notice of you as to exchange blows with you with his own hand. Ye are either very quick or parlous slow at arms."

"It is quick that he is," said Gascoyne, speaking up in his friend's behalf. "For the second time that Falworth delivered the stroke, Sir James could not reach him to return. So I saw it with mine own eyes."

But that very sterling independence that had brought Myles so creditably through this adventure was certain to embroil him with the rude, half-savage lads about him, some who, especially among the bachelors, were his superiors as well in age as in skill and training. As said before, the bachelors had enforced from the younger boys a fagging sort of attendance on their various personal needs, and it was on this point that Myles first came to grief. As it chanced, several days passed before any demand was made upon him for service to the heads of the squirehood, but when that demand was made, the bachelors were very quick to see that the boy who was bold enough to speak up to Sir James Lee was not likely to be a willing fag for them.

"I tell you, Francis," he said, as Gascoyne and he talked over the matter one day—"I tell you I will never serve them. Prithee, what shame can be fouler than to do such menial service, saving for one's rightful lord?"

"Marry!" quoth Gascoyne. "I reason not of shame at this or that. All I know is that others serve them who are as good and maybe better than I, and that if I do not serve them I get knocked in the head therefor."

"I judge not for you," said Myles. "Ye are used to these castle ways, but only I know that I will not serve them, though they be thirty against me instead of thirteen."

"Then you are a fool," said Gascoyne, dryly.

Now in this matter of service there was one thing above all others that stirred Myles Falworth's ill-liking. The winter before he had come to Devlen, Walter Blunt, who was somewhat of a Sybarite in his way, and who had a repugnance to bathing in the general tank in the open armory court in frosty weather, had had Dick Carpenter build a trough in the corner of the dormitory for the use of the bachelors, and every morning it was the duty of the younger squires to bring three pails of water to fill this private tank for the use of the head esquires. It was the sight of two of his fellow squires fetching and carrying this water that Myles disliked so heartily, and every morning his bile was stirred anew.

"Sooner would I die than yield to such vile service," said he.

He did not know how soon his protestations would be put to the test.

One night—it was a week or two after Myles had come to Devlen—Blunt was called to attend the Earl at livery. The livery was the last meal of the day and was served with great pomp and ceremony about nine o'clock at night to the head of the house as he lay in bed. Curfew had not yet rung, and the lads in the squires' quarters were still wrestling and sparring and romping boisterously in and out around the long row of rude cots in the great dormitory as they made ready for the night. Six or eight flaring links in wrought-iron brackets that stood out from the wall threw a great ruddy glare through the barracklike room—a light of all others to romp by. Myles and Gascoyne were engaged in defending the passageway between their two cots against the attack of three other lads. Myles held his sheepskin coverlet rolled up into a ball and balanced in his hand, ready for launching at the head of one of the others as soon as it should rise from behind the shelter of a cot. Just then Walter Blunt, dressed with more than usual care, passed by on his way to the Earl's house. He stopped for a moment and said,

"Perhaps I will not be in until late tonight, Gascoyne, and ye and Falworth may fetch water tomorrow."

Then he was gone. Myles stood staring after his retreating figure with eyes open and mouth agape, still holding the ball of sheepskin balanced in his hand. Gascoyne burst into a helpless laugh at his blank, stupefied face, but the next moment he laid his hand on his friend's shoulder.

"Myles," said he, "ye'll not make trouble, will ye?"

Myles made no answer. He flung down his sheepskin and sat gloomily down on the cot.

"I said that I would sooner die than fetch water for them," said he.

"Aye, aye," said Gascoyne; "but that was spoken in haste."

Myles said nothing, but shook his head.

But, after all, circumstances shape themselves. The next morning when he rose up through the dark waters of sleep it was to feel someone shaking him violently by the shoulder.

"Come," cried Gascoyne, as Myles opened his eyes—"come, time passes, and we are late."

Myles, bewildered with his sudden awakening, and still fuddled with the fumes of sleep, huddled into his doublet and hose, hardly knowing what he was doing; tying a point here and a point there, and slipping his feet into his shoes. Then he hurried after Gascoyne, frowzy, half dressed, and even yet only half awake. It was not until he was fairly out into the fresh air and saw Gascoyne filling the three leather buckets at the tank that he fully awakened to the fact that he was actually doing that hateful service for the bachelors which he had protested he would sooner die than render.

The sun was just rising, gilding the crown of the donjonkeep with a flame of ruddy light. Below, among the lesser buildings, the day was still gray and misty. Only an occasional noise broke the silence of the early morning: a cough from one of the rooms, the rattle of a pot or a pan stirred by some sleepy scullion, the clapping of a door or a shutter, and now and then the crowing of a cock back of the long row of stables—all sounding loud and startling in the fresh dewy stillness.

"Ye have betrayed me," said Myles, harshly, breaking the silence at last. "I knew not what I was doing, or else I would never have come hither. Nevertheless, even though I be come, I will not carry the water for them."

"So be it," said Gascoyne, tartly. "If ye cannot stomach it; let be, and I will carry all three myself. It will take me two journeys, but, thank heaven, I am not so proud as to wish to get me hard knocks for naught." So saying, he picked up two of the buckets and started away across the court for the dormitory.

Then Myles, with a lowering face, snatched up the third, and, hurrying after, gave him his hand with the extra pail. So it was that he came to do service after all.

"Why tarried ye so long?" said one of the older bachelors, roughly, as the two lads emptied the water into the wooden trough. He sat on the edge of the cot, blowzy and untrussed, with his long hair tumbled and disordered.

His dictatorial tone stung Myles to fury. "We tarried no longer than need be," answered he, savagely. "Have we wings to fly withal at your bidding?"

He spoke so loudly that all in the room heard him. The younger squires who were dressing

41

stared in blank amazement, and Blunt sat up suddenly in his cot.

"Why, how now?" he cried. "Answer ye back your betters so pertly, sirrah? By my soul, I have a mind to crack your head with this clog for your unruly talk."

He glared at Myles as he spoke, and Myles glared back again with right good will. Matters might have come to a crisis, only that Gascoyne and Wilkes dragged their friend away before he had opportunity to answer.

"An ill-conditioned knave as ever I did see," glowed Blunt, glaring at him.

"Myles, Myles," said Gascoyne, almost despairingly, "why will ye breed such mischief for yourself? See ye not that ye have got the ill-will of every one of the bachelors, from Walt Blunt to Robin de Ramsey?"

"I care not," said Myles, fiercely, recurring to his grievance. "Heard ye not how the dogs upbraided me before the whole room? That Blunt called me an ill-conditioned knave."

"Marry!" said Gascoyne, laughing, "and so ye are."

CHAPTER · 8

EVERYONE KNOWS the disagreeable, lurking discomfort that follows a quarrel—a discomfort that embitters the very taste of life for the time being. Such was the dull distaste that Myles felt that morning after what had passed in the dormitory. Everyone in the proximity of such an open quarrel feels a reflected constraint, and in Myles' mind was a disagreeable doubt whether that constraint meant disapproval of him or of his late enemies.

It seemed to him that Gascoyne added the last bitter twang to his unpleasant feelings when, half an hour later, they marched with the others to chapel.

"Why do ye breed such trouble for yourself, Myles?" said he, referring to what he had already said. "Is it not foolish for you to come hither to this place, and then not submit to the ways thereof, as the rest of us do?"

"Ye talk not like a true friend to chide me thus," said Myles, sullenly; and he withdrew his arm from his friend's.

"Marry, come up!" said Gascoyne. "If I were not your friend, I would let you jog your own way. It aches not my bones to have yours drubbed."

Just then they entered the chapel, and words that might have led to a quarrel were brought to a close.

Myles was not slow to see that he had the ill-will of the head of their company. That morning in the armory he had occasion to ask some question of Blunt. The head squire stared coldly at him for a moment, gave him a short, gruff answer, and then, turning his back abruptly, began talking with one of the other bachelors. Myles flushed hot at the other's insulting manner, and looked quickly around to see if any of the others had observed what had passed. It was a comfort to him to see that all were too busy arming themselves to think of anything else. Nevertheless, his face was lowering as he turned away.

"Someday I will show him that I am as good a man as he," he muttered to himself. "An evil-hearted dog to put shame upon me!"

The storm was brewing and ready to break.

That day was exceptionally hot and close, and permission had been asked by and granted to those squires not on duty to go down to the river for a bath after exercise at the pels. But as Myles replaced his arms in the rack, a little page came with a bidding to come to Sir James in his office.

"Look now," said Myles, "here is just my ill-fortune. Why might he not have waited an hour longer rather than cause me to miss going with you?"

"Nay," said Gascoyne, "let not that grieve you, Myles. Wilkes and I will wait for you in the dormitory. Will we not, Edmund? Make ye haste and go to Sir James."

Sir James was sitting at the table studying a scroll of parchment when Myles entered his office and stood before him at the table.

"Well, boy," said he, laying aside the parchment and looking up at the lad, "I have tried you fairly for these few days, and may say that I have found you worthy to be entered upon the rolls as esquire of the body."

"I give you thanks, sir," said Myles.

The knight nodded his head in acknowledgment, but did not at once give the word of dismissal that Myles had expected. "D'ye mean to write a letter home soon?" said he, suddenly.

"Aye," said Myles, gaping in great wonderment at the strangeness of the question.

"Then when ye do write," said Sir James, "give my deep regards to your father." Then he continued, after a brief pause, "Him did I know well in times gone by, and we were right true friends in hearty love, and for his sake I would befriend you—that is, in so much as is fitting."

"Sir," said Myles. Sir James held up his hand, and he stopped short in his thanks.

"But, boy," said he, "that which I sent for you to tell you was of more import than these. Do ye know that your father is an attainted outlaw?"

"Nay!" cried Myles, his cheeks blazing up as red as fire. "Who says that of him lies in his teeth."

"Ye mistake me," said Sir James, quietly. "It is sometimes no shame to be outlawed and banned. Had it been so, I would not have told you thereof, nor have bidden you send my true love to your father, as I did but now. But, boy, he stands continually in great danger—greater than ye know. Were it known where he lives hidden, it might be to his undoing and utter ruin. I thought that ye might not know that. And so I sent for you to tell you that it behooves you to say not one single word concerning him to any of these new friends of yours, nor who he is, nor what he is."

"But how came my father to be so banned?" said Myles, in a constrained and husky voice, and after a long time of silence.

"That I may not tell you just now," said the old knight, "only this—that I have been bidden

45

to make it known to you that your father has an enemy full as powerful as my lord the Earl himself, and that through that enemy all his ill-fortune—his blindness and everything—has come. Moreover, did this enemy know where your father lives, he would slay him right speedily."

"Sir," cried Myles, violently smiting his open palm upon the table, "tell me who this man is, and I will kill him!"

Sir James smiled grimly. "Ye talk like a boy," said he. "Wait until ye are grown to be a man. Perhaps then ye may repent you of these bold words, for onetime this enemy of your father's was reckoned the foremost knight in England, and he is now the King's dear friend and a great lord."

"But," said Myles, after another long time of heavy silence, "will not my lord then befriend me for the sake of my father, who was onetime his dear comrade?"

Sir James shook his head. "It may not be," said he. "Neither ye nor your father must look for open favor from the Earl. If he befriended Falworth, and it came to be known that he had given him aid or succor, it might be to his own undoing. No, boy. Ye must not even look to be taken into the household to serve with gentlemen as the other squires serve, but must even live your own life here and fight your own way."

Myles' eyes blazed. "Then," cried he, fiercely, "it is shame and attaint upon my lord the Earl, and cowardice as well, and never will I ask favor of him who is so untrue a friend as to turn his back upon a comrade in trouble as he turns his back upon my father."

"Ye are a foolish boy," said Sir James with a bitter smile, "and know naught of the world. If ye would look for man to befriend man to his own danger, ye must look elsewhere than on this earth. Was I not onetime Mackworth's dear friend as well as your father? It could cost him naught to honor me, and here am I fallen to be a teacher of boys. Go to! You are a fool."

Then, after a little pause of brooding silence, he went on to say that the Earl was no better or worse than the rest of the world. That men of his position had many jealous enemies, ever seeking their ruin, and that such must look first of all each to himself, or else be certainly ruined, and drag down others in that ruin. Myles was silenced, but the bitterness had entered his heart and abided with him for many a day afterward.

Perhaps Sir James read his feelings in his frank face, for he sat looking curiously at him, twirling his grizzled mustache. "Ye are like to have hard knocks of it, lad, before ye have gotten safely through the world," said he, with more kindness in his harsh voice than was usual. "But get ye not into fights before your time." Then he charged the boy very seriously to live at peace with his fellow squires and for his father's sake as well as his own to enter into none of the broils that were so frequent in their quarters.

It was with this special admonition against brawling that Myles was dismissed, to enter, before five minutes had passed, into the first really great fight of his life.

Besides Gascoyne and Wilkes, he found gathered in the dormitory six or eight of the company of squires who were to serve that day upon household duty; among others, Walter Blunt and three other bachelors, who were changing their coarse service clothes for others more fit for the household.

"Why did ye tarry so long?" said Gascoyne as Myles entered. "I thought ye were never coming."

"Where go ye, Falworth?" called Blunt from the other end of the room, where he was lacing his doublet.

Just now Myles had no heart in the swimming or sport of any sort, but he answered, shortly, "I go to the river to swim."

"Nay," said Blunt, "Ye go not forth from the castle today. Have ye forgot how ye did answer me back about fetching the water this morning? This day ye must do penance, so go ye straight to the armory and scour up my breastplate."

From the time he had arisen that morning everything had gone wrong with Myles. He had felt himself already outraged in rendering service to the bachelors, he had quarreled with the head of the squires, he had nearly quarreled with Gascoyne, and then had come the bitterest and worst of all, the knowledge that his father was an outlaw, and that the Earl would not stretch out a hand to aid him or to give him any countenance. Blunt's words brought the last bitter cut to his heart, and they stung him to fury. For a while he could not answer, but stood glaring with a face fairly convulsed with passion at the young man, who continued his toilet, unconscious of the wrath of the new recruit.

Gascoyne and Wilkes, accepting Myles' punishment as a thing of course, were about to leave the dormitory when Myles checked them.

"Stop, Francis!" he cried, hoarsely. "Think ye that I will stay behind to do yonder dog's dirty work? No; I go with you."

A moment or two of dumb, silent amazement followed his bold words. Then Blunt cried, "Are ye mad?"

"Nay," answered Myles in the same hoarse voice, "I am not mad. I tell you a better man than you should not stay me from going if I wish to go."

"I will break your cockerel head for that speech," said Blunt furiously. He stooped as he spoke, and picked up a heavy clog that lay at his feet.

It was no insignificant weapon either. The shoes of those days were sometimes made of cloth and had long pointed toes stuffed with tow or wool. In muddy weather, thick, heavy clogs or wooden soles were strapped, like a skate, to the bottom of the foot. That clog which Blunt had seized was perhaps eighteen or twenty inches long, two or two and a half inches thick at the heel, tapering to a point at the toe. As the older lad advanced, Gascoyne stepped between him and his victim.

"Do not harm him, Blunt," he pleaded. "Bear ye in mind how newcome he is among us. He knows not our ways as yet."

"Stand ye back, Gascoyne," said Blunt, harshly, as he thrust him aside. "I will teach him our ways so that he will not soon forget them."

49

Close to Myles' feet was another clog like the one which Blunt held. Myles snatched it up, and set his back against the wall, with a white face and a heart beating heavily and tumultuously, but with courage steeled to meet the coming encounter. There was a hard, grim look in his blue eyes that, for a moment perhaps, quelled the elder lad. He hesitated. "Tom! Walt! Ned!" he called to the other bachelors, "come hither, and lend me a hand with this knave."

"If ye come nigh me," panted Myles, "I will brain the first within reach."

Then Gascoyne dodged behind the others, and, without being seen, slipped out of the room for help.

The battle that followed was quick, sharp, and short. As Blunt strode forward, Myles struck, and struck with might and main, but he was too excited to deliver his blow with calculation. Blunt parried it with the clog he held, and the next instant, dropping his weapon, gripped Myles tight about the body, pinning his arms to his sides.

Myles also dropped the clog he held, and, wrenching out his right arm with a sudden heave, struck Blunt full in the face, and then with another blow sent him staggering back. It all passed in an instant. The next the three other bachelors were upon him, grabbing him by the body, the arms, the legs. For a moment or two they swayed and stumbled hither and thither, and then down they fell in a struggling heap.

Myles fought like a wildcat, kicking, struggling, scratching; striking with elbows and fists. He caught one of the three by his collar, and tore his jacket open from the neck to the waist. He drove his foot into the pit of the stomach of another, and knocked him breathless. The other lads not in the fight stood on the benches and the beds around, but such was the awe inspired by the prestige of the bachelors that not one of them dared to lend a hand to help him, and so Myles fought his fierce battle alone.

But four to one were odds too great, and though Myles struggled as fiercely as ever, by and by it was with less and less resistance.

Blunt had picked up the clog he had dropped when he first attacked the lad, and now stood over the struggling heap, white with rage, the blood running from his lip, cut and puffed where Myles had struck him, and murder looking out from his face, if ever it looked out of the face of any mortal being.

"Hold him a little," said he, fiercely, "and I will still him for you."

Even yet it was no easy matter for the others to do his bidding, but presently he got his chance and struck a heavy, cruel blow at Myles' head. Myles only partly warded it off with his arm. Hitherto he had fought in silence; now he gave a harsh cry.

"Holy saints!" cried Edmund Wilkes. "They will kill him."

Blunt struck two more blows, both of them upon the body, and then at last they had the poor boy down, with his face upon the ground and his arms pinned to his sides, and Blunt, bracing himself for the stroke, with a grin of rage raised a heavy clog for one terrible blow that should finish the fight.

51

CHAPTER · 9

"How now, messieurs?" said a harsh voice that fell upon the turmoil like a thunderclap, and there stood Sir James Lee. Instantly the struggle ceased, and the combatants scrambled to their feet.

The older lads stood silent before their chief, but Myles was deaf and blind and mad with passion. He knew not where he stood or what he said or did. White as death, he stood for a while glaring about him, catching his breath convulsively. Then he screamed hoarsely.

"Who struck me? Who struck me when I was down? I will have his blood that struck me!" He caught sight of Blunt. "It was he that struck me!" he cried. "Foul traitor! Coward!" and thereupon leaped at his enemy like a wildcat.

"Stop!" cried Sir James Lee, clutching him by the arm.

Myles was too blinded by his fury to see who it was that held him. "I will not stop!" he cried, struggling and striking at the knight. "Let me go! I will have his life that struck me when I was down!"

The next moment he found himself pinned close against the wall, and then, as though his sight came back, he saw the grim face of the old one-eyed knight looking into his.

"Do ye know who I am?" said a stern voice.

Instantly Miles ceased struggling, and his arms fell at his sides. "Aye," he said, in a gasping voice, "I know you."

He swallowed spasmodically for a moment or

two, and then, in the sudden revulsion of feeling, burst out sobbing convulsively.

Sir James marched the two off to his office, he himself walking between them, holding an arm of each, the other lads following behind, awestruck and silent. Entering the office, Sir James shut the door behind him, leaving the group of squires clustered outside about the stone steps, speculating in whispers as to what would be the outcome of the matter.

After Sir James had seated himself, the two standing facing him, he regarded them for a while in silence. "How now, Walter Blunt," said he at last, "what have ye to say?"

"Why, this," said Blunt, wiping his bleeding lip. "That fellow, Myles Falworth, has been breeding mutiny and revolt ever since he came hither among us, and because he was mutinous I would punish him."

"In that ye lie!" burst out Myles. "Never have I been mutinous in my life."

"Be silent, sir," said Sir James, sternly. "I will hear you later."

"Nay," said Myles, with his lips twitching and writhing, "I will not be silent. I am friendless here, and ye are all against me, but I will not be silent and brook to have lies spoken of me."

Even Blunt stood aghast at Myles' boldness. Never had he heard anyone speak so to Sir James before. He did not dare for the moment even to look up. Second after second of dead stillness passed, while Sir James sat looking at Myles with a stern, terrifying calmness that chilled him in spite of the heat of his passion.

"Sir," said the old man at last, in a hard, quiet

voice, "ye know naught of rules and laws of such a place as this. Nevertheless, it is time for ye to learn them. So I will tell you now that if ye open your lips to say only one single word more except at my bidding, I will send you to the black vault of the donjon to cool your hot spirits on bread and water for a week."

There was something in the measured quietness of the old knight's tone that quelled Myles utterly and entirely. A little space of silence followed. "Now then, Blunt," said Sir James, turning to the bachelor, "tell me all the ins and outs of this business with no more underdealing."

This time Blunt's story, though naturally prejudiced in his own favor, was fairly true. Then Myles told his side of the case, the old knight listening attentively.

"Why, how now, Blunt," said Sir James, when Myles had ended. "I myself gave the lads leave to go to the river to bathe. Why should ye forbid one of them?"

"I did it but to punish this fellow for his mutiny," said the bachelor. "I thought we at their head were to have oversight concerning them."

"So ye are," said the knight; "but only to a degree. Before ye take it upon ye to overrule any of my orders or permits, come ye first to me. Do you understand?"

"Aye," answered Blunt, sullenly.

"So be it, and now get ye gone," said the knight; "and let me hear no more of beating out brains with wooden clogs. If ye fight your battles, let there not be murder in them. This is twice that the like has happened. If I hear more of such doings—" He did not utter his threat, but stopped short, and fixed his one eye sternly upon the head squire. "Now shake hands, and be ye friends," said he, abruptly.

Blunt made a motion to obey, but Myles put his hand behind him.

"Nay, I shake not hands with anyone who struck me while I was down."

"So be it," said the knight, grimly. "Now ye may go, Blunt. Falworth, stay; I would speak to you further."

"Tell me," said he, when the elder lad had left them, "why will ye not serve these bachelors as the other squires do? Such is the custom here. Why will ye not obey it?"

"Because," said Myles, "I cannot stomach it, and they shall not make me serve them. If ye bid me do it, sir, I will do it; but not at their command."

"Nay," said the knight, "I do not bid you do them service. That lies with you, to render or not, as ye see fit. But how can ye hope to fight single-handed against the commands of a dozen lads all older and mightier than you?"

"I know not," said Myles; "but were they a hundred, instead of thirteen, they should not make me serve them."

"Ye are a fool!" said the old knight, smiling faintly, "for that be not courage, but folly. When one sets about righting a wrong, one drives not full head against it, for in so doing one gets naught but hard knocks. Nay, go deftly about it, and then, when the time is ripe, strike the blow. Now our beloved King Henry, when he was the Earl of Derby, what could he have gained had he stood so against the old King

Richard, brooking the King face to face? I tell you he would have been knocked on the head as ye were like to have been this day. Now were I you, and had to fight a fight against odds, I would first get me friends behind me, and then—" He stopped short, but Myles understood him well enough.

"Sir," said he, with a gulp, "I do thank you for your friendship, and ask your pardon for doing as I did."

"I grant you pardon," said the knight, "but tell you plainly, if ye face me so again, I will truly send thee to the black cell for a week. Now get ye away."

All the other lads were gone when Myles came forth, save only the faithful Gascoyne, who sacrificed his bath that day to stay with his friend. And perhaps that little act of self-denial moved Myles more than many a great thing might have done.

"It was right kind of you, Francis," said he, laying his hand affectionately on his friend's shoulder. "I know not why ye love me so."

"Why, for one thing, this matter," answered his friend; "because I think ye are the best fighter and the bravest one of all of us squires."

Myles laughed. Nevertheless, Gascoyne's words were a soothing balm for much that had happened that day.

"I will fight me no more just now," said he.

And then he told his friend all that Sir James had advised about biding his time.

Gascoyne blew a long whistle. "Beshrew me!" said he, "but I think old Bruin is on your side of the quarrel, Myles. If that be so, I am with you also, and others that I can name as well."

"So be it," said Myles. "Then am I content to bide the time when we may become strong enough to stand against them."

CHAPTER · 10

PERHAPS THERE IS NOTHING more delightful in the romance of boyhood than the finding of some secret hiding place whither a body may creep away from the bustle of the world's life, to nestle in quietness for an hour or two. More especially is such delightful if it happens that, by peeping from out it one may look down upon the bustling matters of busy everyday life, while one lies snugly hidden away unseen by any, as though one were in some strange, invisible world of one's own.

Such a hiding place as would have filled the heart of almost any boy with sweet delight Myles and Gascoyne found one summer afternoon. They called it their Eyry, and the name suited well for the roosting place of the young hawks that rested in its windy stillness, looking down upon the shifting castle life in the courts below.

Behind the north stable, a great, long, rambling building, thick-walled and black with age, lay an older part of the castle than that peopled by the better class of life—a cluster of great thick walls, rudely but strongly built, now the dwelling place of stableboys and cattle, swine, and poultry. From one part of these ancient walls, and fronting an inner court of the castle, arose a tall, circular, heavy-buttressed tower, considerably higher than the other buildings, and so mantled with a dense growth of aged ivy as to stand a shaft of solid green. Above its crumbling crown circled hundreds of pigeons, white and pied, clapping and clattering in noisy flight through the sunny air. Several windows, some closed with shutters, peeped here and there from out the leaves, and near the top of the pile was a row of arched openings, as though a balcony or an airy gallery.

Myles had more than once felt an idle curiosity about this tower, and one day, as he and Gascoyne sat together, he pointed his finger and said, "What is that place?"

"That," answered Gascoyne, looking over his shoulder—"that they call Brutus Tower, for they do say that Brutus built it when he came to Britain. I believe not the tale myself; nevertheless it is marvelous ancient, and old Robin-the-Fletcher tells me that there are stairways built in the wall and passageways, and a maze wherein a body may get lost, if he knows not the way, and never see the blessed light of day again."

"Marry," said Myles, "those are strange sayings. Who lives there now?"

"No one lives there," said Gascoyne, "excepting some of the stableboys and that halfwitted gooseherd who flung stones at us yesterday when we mocked him down in the paddock. He and his wife and those others dwell in the vaults beneath, like rabbits. No one else has lived there since Earl Robert's day, which was a hundred years ago. The story goes that Earl Robert's brother—or stepbrother—was murdered there, and some men say by the Earl himself. Since that day it has been tight shut."

Myles stared at the tower for a while in silence. "It is a strange-seeming place from without," said he at last, "and it may be even more strange inside. Have you ever been within, Francis?"

"Nay," said Gascoyne; "did I not say it has been fast locked since Earl Robert's day?"

"By Our Lady," said Myles, "if I had lived here in this place as long as ye, I would have been within it before this."

"Beshrew me," said Gascoyne, "but I have never thought of such a matter." He turned and looked at the tall crown rising into the warm sunlight with a new interest, for the thought of entering it smacked pleasantly of adventure. "How would ye set about getting within?" said he presently.

"Why, look," said Myles; "see ye not yonder hole in the ivy branches? I think there is a window at that place. If I mistake not, it is within reach of the stable eaves. A person might climb up by the fagot pile to the roof of the hen house and then by the long stable to the north stable, and so to that hole."

Gascoyne looked thoughtfully at the Brutus

Tower, and then suddenly inquired, "Would ye go there?"

"Aye," said Myles briefly.

"So be it. Lead ye the way in the venture. I will follow after you," said Gascoyne.

As Myles had said, the climbing from roof to roof was a matter easy enough for an active pair of lads like themselves. But when, by and by, they reached the wall of the tower itself, they found the hidden window much higher from the roof than they had judged from below—perhaps ten or twelve feet—and it was, besides, beyond the eaves and out of their reach.

Myles looked up and looked down. Above was the bushy thickness of the ivy, the branches as thick as a woman's wrist, knotted and intertwined; below was the stone pavement of a narrow inner court between two stable buildings.

"I think I can climb to yonder place," said he.

"Ye'll break your neck," said Gascoyne, hastily.

"Nay," quoth Myles. "I think not. But break or make, we get not there without trying. So here goes for the venture."

"Ye are a harebrained knave as ever drew breath of life," said Gascoyne, "and will cause me to come to grief some of these fine days. Nevertheless, if ye be Jack Fool and lead the way, go, and I will be Tom Fool and follow. If your neck is worth so little, mine is worth no more."

It was indeed a perilous climb, but that special providence which guards reckless lads befriended them. So, by climbing from one knotted, clinging stem to another, they were presently seated snugly in the ivied niche in the window. It was barred from within by a crumbling shutter. The rusty fastening, after some little effort upon the part of the two, gave way, and entering the narrow opening, they found themselves in a small triangular passageway from which a steep flight of stone steps led down through a hollow in the massive wall to the room below.

At the bottom of the steps was a heavy oaken door, which stood ajar, hanging upon a single rusty hinge, and from the room within a dull, gray light glimmered faintly. Myles pushed the door farther open. It creaked and grated horribly on its rusty hinge, and as in instant answer to the discordant shriek came a faint piping squeaking, a rustling and a pattering of soft footsteps.

"The ghosts!" cried Gascoyne, in a quavering whisper, and for a moment Myles felt the chill of gooseflesh creep up and down his spine. But the next moment he laughed.

"Nay," said he, "they are rats. Look at yonder fellow, Francis! He's as big as Mother Joan's kitten. Give me that stone." He flung it at the rat. It flew clattering across the floor. There was another pattering rustle of hundreds of feet, and then a breathless silence.

The boys stood looking around them, and a strange enough sight it was. The room was a perfect circle of about twenty feet across, and was piled high with an indistinguishable mass of lumber—rude tables, ruder chairs, ancient chests, bits and remnants of cloth and sacking and leather, old helmets and pieces of armor of a bygone time, broken spears and poleaxes, pots and pans and kitchenware of all sorts and kinds.

A straight beam of sunlight fell through a broken shutter like a bar of gold, falling upon the floor in a long streak of dazzling light that illuminated the whole room with a yellow glow.

"By Our Lady!" said Gascoyne at last, in a hushed voice. "Here is Father Time's garret for sure. Did ye ever see the like, Myles? Look at yonder arbalest. Sure Brutus himself used such a one!"

"Nay," said Myles; "but look at this saddle. Marry, here be a rat's nest in it."

Clouds of dust rose as they rummaged among the moldering mass, setting them coughing and sneezing. Now and then a great gray rat would shoot out beneath their very feet, and disappear, like a sudden shadow, into some hole or cranny in the wall.

"Come," said Myles at last, brushing the dust from his jacket, "if we tarry here longer we will have chance to see no other sights. The sun is falling low."

An arched stairway upon the opposite side of the room from which they had entered wound upward through the wall, the stone steps being lighted by narrow slits of windows cut through the massive masonry. Above the room they had just left was another of the same shape and size, but with an oak floor, sagging and rising into hollows and hills, where the joist had rotted away beneath. It was bare and empty, and not even a rat was to be seen. Above was another room; above that, another—all the passages and stairways which connected the one story with the other being built in the wall, which, where solid, was perhaps fifteen feet thick.

From the third floor a straight flight of steps led upward to a closed door from the other side of which shone the dazzling brightness of sunlight, and whence came a strange noise—a soft rustling, a melodious murmur. The boys put their shoulders against the door, which was fastened, and pushed with might and main—once, twice. Suddenly the lock gave way, and out they pitched headlong into a blaze of sunlight. A deafening clapping and uproar sounded in their ears, and scores of pigeons, suddenly disturbed, rose in stormy flight.

They sat up and looked around them in silent wonder. They were in a bower of leafy green. It was the top story of the tower, the roof of which had crumpled and toppled in, leaving it open to the sky, with only here and there a slanting beam or two supporting a portion of the tiled roof, affording shelter for the nests of the pigeons crowded closely together. Over everything the ivy had grown in a mantling sheet —a network of shimmering green through which the sunlight fell flickering.

"This passes wonder," said Gascoyne, at last, breaking the silence.

"Aye," said Myles. "I did never see the like in all my life." Then, "Look, yonder is a room beyond. Let us see what it is, Francis."

Entering an arched doorway, the two found themselves in a beautiful little vaulted chapel, about eighteen feet long and twelve or fifteen wide. It comprised the crown of one of the massive buttresses, and from it opened the row of arched windows which could be seen from below through the green shimmering of the ivy leaves. The boys pushed aside the trailing tendrils and looked out and down. The whole castle lay spread below them, with the busy people unconsciously intent upon the matters of their daily work. They could see the gardener, with bowed back, patiently working among the flowers in the garden, the stableboys grooming the horses, a bevy of ladies in the privy garden playing at shuttlecock with battledores of wood; a group of gentlemen walking up and down in front of the Earl's house. They could see the household servants hurrying hither and thither, two little scullions at fisticuffs, and a kitchen girl standing in the doorway scratching her head.

It was all like a puppet show of real life, each acting unconsciously a part in the play. The cool wind came in through the rustling leaves and fanned their cheeks, hot with the climb up the winding stairway.

"We will call it our Eyry," said Gascoyne, "and we will be the hawks that live here." And that was how it got its name.

The next day Myles had the armorer make him a score of large spikes, which he and Gascoyne drove between the ivy branches and into the cement of the wall, and so made a safe passageway by which to reach the window niche in the wall.

CHAPTER · 11

THE TWO FRIENDS kept the secret of the Eyry to themselves for a little while, now and then visiting the old tower to rummage among the lumber stored in the lower room, or to loiter away the afternoon in the windy solitudes of the upper heights. And in that little time, when the ancient keep was to them a small world unknown to any but themselves—a world far away above all the dull matters of everyday life—they talked of many things that might never have been known to one another. Mostly they spoke the crude romantic thoughts and desires of boyhood's time —chaff thrown to the wind, in which, however, lay a few stray seeds, fated to fall to good earth, and to ripen to fruition in manhood's day.

In the intimate talks of that time Myles imparted something of his honest solidity to Gascoyne's somewhat weathercock nature. And to Myles' ruder and more uncouth character Gascoyne lent a tone of his gentler manners, learned in his pagehood service as attendant upon the Countess and her ladies.

In other things, also, the character and experience of the one lad helped to supply what was lacking in the other. Myles was replete with old Latin gestes, fables, and sermons picked up during his school life, in those intervals of his more serious studies when Prior Edward had permitted him to browse in the greener pastures of the *Gesta Romanorum* and the *Disciplina Clericalis* of the monastery library. Gascoyne was never weary of hearing him tell those marvelous stories culled from the crabbed Latin of the old manuscript volumes.

Upon his part Gascoyne was full of the lore of the waiting room and the antechamber, and Myles, who in all his life had never known a lady, young or old, except his mother, was never tired of lying silently listening to Gascoyne's chatter of the gay doings of the castle gentle life, in which he had taken part so often in the merry days of his pagehood.

"I do wonder," said Myles, quaintly, "that ye could ever find the courage to bespeak a young maid, Francis. Never did I do so, nor ever could. Rather would I face three strong men than one young damsel."

Whereupon Gascoyne burst out laughing. "Marry!" quoth he, "they are not such terrible things, but gentle and pleasant-spoken, and soft and smooth as any cat."

"No matter for that," said Myles. "I would not face one such for worlds."

It was during the short time when, so to speak, the two owned the solitude of the Brutus Tower that Myles told his friend of his father's outlawry and of the peril in which the family stood.

"I do marvel," said Gascoyne one day, as the two lay stretched in the Eyry, looking down into the castle courtyard below—"I do marvel, now that ye are established here this month and more, that my lord never has you called to service upon household duty. Can ye riddle me why it is so, Myles?"

The subject was a very sore one with Myles. Until Sir James had told him of the matter in his office that day he had never known that his father was attainted and outlawed. He had accepted the change from their earlier state and the bald poverty of their life at Crosbey-Dale with the easy carelessness of boyhood. Sir James' words were the first to awaken him to a realization of the misfortunes of the house of Falworth. His was a brooding nature, and in the three or four weeks that passed he had meditated so much over what had been told him that by and by it almost seemed as if a shadow of shame rested upon his father's fair name, even though the attaint set upon him was unrighteous and unjust, as Myles knew it must be. He had felt angry and resentful at the Earl's neglect. As days passed and he was not noticed in any way, his heart was at times very bitter.

So now Gascoyne's innocent question touched a sore spot. Myles spoke with a sharp, angry pain in his voice that made the other look up quickly. "Sooner would my lord have yonder swineherd serve him in the household than me," said he.

"Why may that be, Myles?" said Gascoyne.

"Because," answered Myles, with the same angry bitterness in his voice, "either the Earl is a coward that fears to befriend me, or else he is a caitiff, ashamed of his own flesh and blood, and of me, the son of his onetime comrade."

Gascoyne raised himself on his elbow and opened his eyes wide in wonderment. "Afraid of you, Myles!" said he. "Why should he be afraid to befriend thee? Who are ye that the Earl should fear thee?"

Myles hesitated for a moment or two. Wisdom bade him remain silent upon the dangerous topic, but his heart yearned for sympathy and companionship in his trouble. "I will tell you," said he, suddenly, and therewith poured out all of the story, so far as he knew it, to his listening, wondering friend. His heart felt lighter to be thus eased of its burden. "And now," said he, as he concluded, "is not this Earl a mean-hearted caitiff to leave me, the son of his one-time friend and kinsman, thus to stand or to fall alone among strangers and in a strange place without once stretching me a helping hand?"

He waited, and Gascoyne knew that he expected an answer.

"I know not that he is a mean-hearted caitiff, Myles," said he at last, hesitatingly. "The Earl has many enemies, and I have heard that he has stood more than once in peril, having been accused of dealings with the King's foes. He was cousin to the Earl of Kent, and I do remember hearing that he had a narrow escape at that time from ruin. There be more reasons than ye know why he should not have dealings with your father."

"I had not thought," said Myles bitterly, after a little pause, "that ye would stand up for him and against me in this quarrel, Gascoyne. Him will I never forgive so long as I may live, and I had thought that ye would have stood by me."

"So I do," said Gascoyne, hastily, "and do love you more than anyone in all the world, Myles. But I had thought that it would make you feel more easy to think that the Earl was not against you. Indeed, from all ye have told me, I truly think that he and Sir James mean to befriend you and hold you privately in kind regard."

"Then why does he not stand forth like a man

and befriend me and my father openly, even if it be to his own peril?" said Myles, reverting stubbornly to what he had first spoken.

Gascoyne did not answer, but lay for a long while in silence. "Know ye," he suddenly asked, after a while, "who is this great enemy of whom Sir James speaks, and who seeks to drive your father to ruin?"

"Nay," said Myles, "I know not, for my father has never spoken of these things, and Sir James would not tell me. But this I know," said he, suddenly, grinding his teeth together, "if I do not hunt him out someday and slay him like a dog—" He stopped abruptly, and Gascoyne, looking at him, saw that his eyes were full of tears, whereupon he turned his look away again quickly, and fell to shooting pebbles out through the open window with his finger and thumb.

"Ye will tell no one of these things that I have said?" asked Myles, after a while.

"Not I," said Gascoyne. "Think ye I could do such a thing?"

"Nay," said Myles briefly.

Perhaps this talk more than anything else that had ever passed between them knit the two friends the closer together, for, as I have said, Myles felt easier now that he had poured out his bitter thoughts and words. As for Gascoyne, I think that there is nothing so flattering to one's soul as to be made the confidant of a stronger nature.

But the old tower served another purpose than that of a spot in which to pass away a few idle hours, or in which to indulge the confidences of

70

friendship, for it was there that Myles gathered a backing of strength for resistance against the tyranny of the bachelors. And it is for that more than for any other reason that it has been told how they found the place and of what they did there, feeling secure against interruption.

Myles Falworth was not of a kind that forgets or neglects a thing upon which the mind has once been set. Perhaps his chief objective since the talk with Sir James following his fight in the dormitory had been successful resistance to the exactions of the head of the body of squires. He was now (more than a month had passed) looked upon by nearly if not all of the younger lads as an acknowledged leader in his own class. So one day he broached a matter to Gascoyne that had for some time been digesting in his mind. It was the formation of a secret order, calling themselves the "Knights of the Rose," their meeting place to be the chapel of the Brutus Tower, and their object to be the righting of wrongs, "as they," said Myles, "of Arthur and his Round Table did right wrongs."

"But, pray, what wrongs are there to right in this place?" asked Gascoyne, after listening intently to the plan which Myles set forth.

"Why, first of all, this," said Myles, clinching his fists, as he had a habit of doing when anything stirred him deeply, "that we set those vile bachelors to their right place; and that is, that they be no longer our masters, but our fellows."

Gascoyne shook his head. He hated clashing and conflict above all things, and was for peace. Why should they thus rush to thrust themselves into trouble? Let matters abide as they were a little longer. Surely life was pleasant enough without turning it all topsy-turvy. Then, with a sort of indignation, why should Myles, who had only come among them a month, take such service more to heart than they who had endured it for years? And, finally, with the hopefulness of so many of the rest of us, he advised Myles to let matters alone, and they would right themselves in time.

But Myles' mind was determined. His active spirit could not brook resting passively under a wrong. He would endure no longer, and now or never they must make their stand.

"But look ye, Myles Falworth," said Gascoyne, "all this is not to be done without fighting shrewdly. Will ye take that fighting upon your own self? As for me, I tell you I love it not."

"Why, aye," said Myles; "I ask no man to do what I will not do myself."

Gascoyne shrugged his shoulders. "So be it," said he. "If ye have appetite to run your head against hard knocks, do it in mercy's name!"

There was a spirit of drollery in Gascoyne's speech that rubbed against Myles' earnestness.

"Out upon it!" cried he, his patience giving way. "See ye not that I am in serious earnest? Why then do ye still jest like Mad Noll, my lord's fool? If ye will not lend me your aid in this matter, say so and have done with it, and I will bethink me of somewhere else to turn."

Then Gascoyne yielded at once, as he always did when his friend lost his temper, and having once assented to it, entered into the scheme heart and soul. Three other lads—one of them that tall, thin squire Edmund Wilkes before spoken of—were sounded upon the subject. They also entered into the plan of the secret organization with an enthusiasm which might perhaps not have been quite so glowing had they realized how very soon Myles intended embarking upon active practical operations. One day Myles and Gascoyne showed them the strange things that they had discovered in the old tower—the inner staircases, the winding passageways, the queer niches and cupboard, and the black shaft of a well that pierced down into the solid wall, and whence, perhaps, the old castle folk had onetime drawn their supply of water in time of siege. And with every new wonder of the marvelous place the enthusiasm of the three recruits rose higher and higher. They rummaged through the lumber pile in the great circular room as Myles and Gascoyne had done, and at last, tired out, they ascended to the airy chapel, and there sat cooling themselves in the rustling freshness of the breeze that came blowing briskly in through the arched windows.

It was then and there that the five discussed and finally determined upon the detailed plans of their organization, canvassing the list of the squirehood, and selecting from it a sufficient number of bold and daring spirits to make up a roll of twenty names in all.

Gascoyne had, as I said, entered into the matter with spirit, and perhaps it was owing more to him than to any other that the project caught its delightful flavor of romance.

"Perchance," said he, as the five lads lay in the rustling stillness through which sounded the monotonous and ceaseless cooing of the pigeons—

"perchance there may be dwarfs and giants and dragons and enchanters and evil knights and what not even nowadays. And who knows but that if we Knights of the Rose hold together we may go forth into the world, and do battle with them, and save beautiful ladies, and have tales and gestes written about us as they are written about the Seven Champions and Arthur and his Round Table."

Perhaps Myles, who lay silently listening to all that was said, was the only one who looked upon the scheme at all in the light of real utility, but I think that even with him the fun of the matter outweighed the serious part.

So it was that the Sacred Order of the Twenty Knights of the Rose came to be initiated. They appointed a code of secret passwords and countersigns which were very difficult to remember, and which were used only when they might excite the curiosity of the other and uninitiated boys by their mysterious sound. They elected Myles as their Grand High Commander, and held secret meetings in the ancient tower, where many mysteries were soberly enacted.

Of course in a day or two all the body of squires knew nearly everything concerning the Knights of the Rose and of their secret meetings in the old tower. The lucky twenty were the objects of envy of all not so fortunate as to be included in this number, and there was a marked air of secrecy about everything they did that appealed to every romantic notion of the youngsters looking on. What was the stormy outcome of it all is now presently to be told.

CHAPTER · 12

THUS IT WAS that Myles, with an eye to open war with the bachelors, gathered a following to his support. It was some little while before matters were brought to a crisis—a week or ten days. Perhaps even Myles had no great desire to hasten matters. He knew that whenever war was declared, he himself would have to bear the brunt of the battle, and even the bravest man hesitates before deliberately thrusting himself into a fight.

One morning Myles and Gascoyne and Wilkes sat under the shade of two trees, between which was a board nailed to the trunks, making a rude bench—always a favorite lounging place for the lads in idle moments. Myles was polishing his basinet with lard and wood ashes, rubbing the metal with a piece of leather, and wiping it clean with a fustian rag. The other two, who had just been relieved from household duty, lay at length idly looking on.

Just then one of the smaller pages, a boy of twelve or thirteen, by name Robin Ingoldsby, crossed the court. He had been crying. His face was red and blubbered, and his body was still shaken with convulsive sniffs.

Myles looked up. "Come hither, Robin," he called from where he sat. "What is it?"

The little fellow came slowly up to where the three rested in the shade. "Mowbray beat me with a strap," said he, rubbing his sleeve across his eyes and catching his breath at the memory.

"Beat you, did ye say?" said Myles, drawing

his brows together. "Why did he beat you?"

"Because," said Robin, "I tarried overlong in fetching a pot of beer from the buttery for him and Wyatt." Then, with a boy's sudden and easy quickness in forgetting past troubles, "Tell me, Falworth," said he, "when will ye give me that knife ye promised me—the one whose blade ye broke yesterday?"

"I know not," said Myles, bluntly, vexed that the boy did not take the disgrace of his beating more to heart. "Sometime soon, mayhap. I think ye should think more of your beating than of a broken knife. Now get ye to your business."

The youngster lingered for a moment or two watching Myles at his work. "What is that on the leather scrap, Falworth?" said he, curiously.

"Lard and ashes," said Myles, testily. "Get thee gone, I say, or I will crack your head for you." And he picked up a block of wood with a threatening gesture.

The youngster made a hideous grimace, and then scurried away, ducking his head, lest in spite of Myles' well-known good nature the block should come whizzing after him.

"Hear ye that now!" cried Myles, flinging down the block again and turning to his two friends. "Beaten with straps because he would not fetch and carry quickly enough to please the haste of these bachelors. Oh, this passes patience, and I, for one, will bear it no longer."

"Nay, Miles," said Gascoyne, soothingly, "the little imp is as lazy as a dormouse and as mischievous as a monkey. I'll warrant the hiding was his due, and that more of the like would do him good."

"Why, how ye do talk, Francis!" said Myles, turning upon him indignantly. "Ye know that ye like to see the boy beaten no more than I." Then, after a pause, "How many, think ye, we muster of our company of the Rose today?"

Wilkes looked doubtfully at Gascoyne. "There be only seventeen of us here now," said he at last. "Brinton and Lambourne are away to Roby Castle with Lord George, and will not be back till Saturday next. And Watt Newton is in the infirmary."

"Seventeen be enough," said Myles, grimly. "Let us get together this afternoon, such as may, in the Brutus Tower, for I, as I did say, will no longer suffer these vile bachelors."

Gascoyne and Wilkes exchanged looks, and then the former blew a long whistle.

So that afternoon a gloomy set of young faces were gathered together in the Eyry—the Knights of the Rose—and all knew why they were assembled. The talk which followed was conducted mostly by Myles. He addressed the others with a straightforward vim and earnestness, but the response was only half-hearted, and when at last, having heated himself up with his own fire, he sat down, puffing out his red cheeks and glaring round, a space of silence followed, the lads looking doubtfully at one another. Myles felt the chill of their silence strike coldly on his enthusiasm, and it vexed him.

"What would ye do, Falworth?" said one of the knights at last. "Would ye have us open a quarrel with the bachelors?"

"Nay," said Miles, gruffly. "I had thought that

ye would all lend me a hand in a pitched battle, but now I see that ye have no stomach for that. Nevertheless, I tell ye plainly I will not submit longer to the bachelors. So now I will ask ye not to take any venture upon yourselves, but only this: that ye will stand by me when I do my fighting, and not let five or seven of them fall upon me at once."

"There is Walter Blunt; he is exceeding strong," said one of the others, after a time of silence. "He could conquer any two of us."

"Nay," said Myles; "ye do fear him too greatly. I tell ye I fear not to stand up to try battle with him, and will do so, too, if the need arise. Only say ye that ye will stand by my back."

"Marry," said Gascoyne, quaintly, "if ye'll dare take the heavy end upon thee, I for one am willing to stand by and see that ye have your fill of fighting."

"I too will stand by you, Myles," said Wilkes.

"And I, and I, and I," said others, chiming in.

Those who would have held back were carried along by the stream, and so it was settled that if the need should arise for Myles to do a bit of fighting, the others should stand by to see that he had fair play.

"When think ye that ye will take your stand against them, Myles?" asked Wilkes.

Myles hesitated a moment. "Tomorrow," said he, grimly.

Several of the lads whistled softly.

Gascoyne was prepared for an early opening of the war, but perhaps not for such an early opening as this. "By Our Lady, Myles, ye are hungry for brawling," said he.

CHAPTER · 13

After the first excitement of meeting, discussing, and deciding had passed, Myles began to feel the weight of the load he had so boldly taken upon himself. He began to reckon what a serious thing it was for him to stand as a single champion against the tyranny that had grown so strong through years of custom. Had he let himself do so, he might almost have repented, but it was too late now for repentance. He had laid his hand to the plow, and he must drive the furrow.

Somehow the news of impending battle had leaked out among the rest of the body of squires, and a buzz of suppressed excitement hummed through the dormitory that evening. The bachelors, to whom, no doubt, vague rumors had been blown, looked lowering, and talked together in low voices, standing apart in a group. Some of them made a rather marked show of secreting knives in the straw of their beds, and no doubt it had its effect upon more than one young heart that secretly thrilled at the sight of the shining blades. However, all was undisturbed that evening. The lights were put out, and the lads retired with more than usual quietness, only for the murmur of whispering.

All night Myles' sleep was more or less disturbed by dreams in which he was now conquering, now being conquered, and before the day had fairly broken he was awake. He lay upon his cot, keying himself up for the encounter which he had set upon himself to face, and it would not be the truth to say that the sight of those knives hidden in the straw the night before had made no impression upon him. By and by he knew the others were beginning to awake, for he heard them softly stirring, and as the light grew broad and strong, saw them arise, one by one, and begin dressing in the gray morning. Then he himself rose and put on his doublet and hose, strapping his belt tightly about his waist; then he sat down on the side of his cot.

Presently that happened for which he was waiting. Two of the younger squires started to bring the bachelors' morning supply of water. As they crossed the room Myles called to them in a loud voice—a little uneven, perhaps:

"Stop! We draw no more water for anyone in this house, saving only for ourselves. Set ye down those buckets, and go back to your places!"

The two lads stopped, half turned, and then stood still, holding the three buckets undecidedly.

In a moment all was uproar and confusion, for by this time every one of the lads had arisen, some sitting on the edge of their beds, some nearly, others quite, dressed. A half-dozen of the Knights of the Rose came over to where Myles stood, gathering in a body behind him, and the others followed, one after another.

The bachelors were hardly prepared for such prompt and vigorous action.

"What is this?" cried one of them, who stood near the two lads with the buckets. "Why fetch ye not the water?"

"Falworth says we shall not fetch it," answered one of the lads, a boy by the name of Gosse.

"What mean ye by that, Falworth?" the young man called to Myles.

Myles' heart was beating thickly and heavily, but nevertheless he spoke up boldly enough. "I mean," said he, "that from henceforth ye shall fetch and carry for yourselves."

"Look'ee, Blunt," called the bachelor; "here is Falworth says the squires will fetch no more water for us."

The head bachelor had heard all that had passed, and was even then hastily slipping on his doublet and hose. "Now, then, Falworth," said he at last, striding forward, "what is this? Ye will fetch no more water, eh? By Our Lady, I will know the reason why."

He was still advancing toward Myles, with two or three of the older bachelors at his heels, when Gascoyne spoke.

"Ye had best stand back, Blunt," said he, "else ye may be hurt. We will not have ye bang Falworth again as ye once did, so stand ye back!"

Blunt stopped short and looked at the lads standing behind Myles, some of them with faces a trifle pale perhaps, but all grim and determined-looking. Then he turned upon his heel suddenly, and walked back to the far end of the dormitory, where the bachelors were presently clustered together. A few words passed between them, and then the thirteen began at once arming themselves, some with wooden clogs and some with the knives which they had so openly concealed the night before. At the sign of im-

minent battle, all those not actively interested
scuttled away to right and left, climbing up on
the benches and cots, and leaving a free field to
the combatants. The next moment would have
brought bloodshed.

Now Myles, thanks to the training of the Crosbey-Dale smith, felt tolerably sure that in a wrestling bout he was a match—perhaps more than a
match—for any one of the body of squires, and
he had determined, if possible, to bring the battle to a single-handed encounter upon that
footing. Accordingly he suddenly stepped forward before the others.

"Look'ee, fellow," he called to Blunt, "ye are
he who struck me while I was down some while
since. Will ye let this quarrel stand between
you and me, and meet me man to man without
weapon? See, I throw down my own, and will
meet you with bare hands." And as he spoke,
he tossed the clog he held in his hand back
upon the cot.

"So be it," said Blunt, with great readiness,
tossing down a similar weapon which he himself held.

"Do not go, Myles," cried Gascoyne. "He is a
villain and a traitor, and would betray you to
your death. I saw him hide a knife in his
doublet."

"You lie!" said Blunt. "I swear, by my faith, I
be barehanded as ye see me! Your friend ac-
cuses me, Myles Falworth, because he knows ye
are afraid of me."

"There ye lie most vilely!" exclaimed Myles.
"Swear ye have no knife, and I will meet you."

"Have ye not heard me say that I have no

knife?" said Blunt. "What more would ye have?"

"Then I will meet you halfway," said Myles.

Gascoyne caught him by the sleeve, and would have withheld him, assuring him that he had seen the bachelor conceal a knife. But Myles, hot for the fight, broke away from his friend without listening to him.

As the two advanced steadily toward each other a breathless silence fell upon the dormitory, in sharp contrast to the uproar and confusion that had filled it a moment before. The lads, standing some upon benches, some upon beds, all watched with breathless interest the meeting of the two champions.

As they approached each other they stopped and stood for a moment a little apart, glaring the one upon the other. They seemed ill enough matched; Blunt was fully half a head taller than Myles, and was thickset and close-knit in young manhood. Nothing but Myles' undaunted pluck could have led him to dare to face an enemy so much older and stouter than himself.

The pause was for only a moment. They who looked saw Blunt slide his hand furtively toward his bosom. Myles saw, too, and in the flash of an instant knew what the gesture meant, and sprang upon the other before the hand could grasp what it sought. As he clutched his enemy he felt what he had in that instant expected to feel—the handle of a dagger. The next moment he cried in a loud voice:

"Oh, you villain! Help, Gascoyne! He has a knife under his doublet!"

In answer to his cry for help, Myles' friends started to his aid. But the bachelors shouted,

"Stand back and let them fight it out alone, else we will knife ye, too." And as they spoke, some of them leaped from the benches whereon they stood, drawing their knives and flourishing them.

For just a few seconds Myles' friends stood cowed, and in those few seconds the fight came to an end with a suddenness unexpected to all.

A struggle fierce and silent followed between the two; Blunt striving to draw his knife, and Myles, with the energy of despair, holding him tightly by the wrist. It was in vain the elder lad writhed and twisted. He was strong enough to overbear Myles, but still was not able to clutch the haft of his knife.

"Ye shall not draw it!" gasped Myles at last. "Ye shall not stab me!"

Then again some of his friends started forward to his aid, but they were not needed, for before they came, the fight was over.

Blunt, finding that he was not able to draw the weapon, suddenly ceased his endeavors, and flung his arms around Myles, trying to bear him down upon the ground, and in that moment his battle was lost.

In an instant—so quick, so sudden, so unexpected that no one could see how it happened—his feet were whirled away from under him, he spun with flying arms across Myles' loins, and pitched with a thud upon the stone floor, where he lay still, motionless, while Myles, his face white with passion and his eyes gleaming, stood glaring around like a young wild boar beset by the dogs.

The next moment the silence was broken, and the uproar broke forth with redoubled violence.

The bachelors, leaping from the benches, came hurrying forward on one side and Myles' friends from the other.

"Ye shall smart for this, Falworth," said one of the older lads. "Perhaps ye have slain him!"

Myles turned upon the speaker like a flash, and with such a passion of fury in his face that the other, a fellow nearly a head taller than he, shrank back, cowed in spite of himself. Then Gascoyne came and laid his hand on his friend's shoulder.

"Who touches me?" cried Myles, hoarsely, turning sharply upon him; and then, seeing who it was, "Oh, Francis, they would have killed me!"

"Come away, Myles," said Gascoyne; "ye know not what ye do. Ye are mad. Come away. What if ye had killed him?"

The words brought Myles somewhat to himself. "I care not!" said he, but sullenly and not passionately, and then he suffered Gascoyne and Wilkes to lead him away.

Meantime Blunt's friends had turned him over, and, after feeling his temples, his wrist, and his heart, bore him away to a bench at the far end of the room. There they fell to chafing his hands and sprinkling water in his face, a crowd of the others gathering about. Blunt was hidden from Myles by those who stood around, and the lad listened to the broken talk that filled the room with its confusion, his anxiety growing keener as he became cooler. But at last, with a heartfelt joy, he gathered from the confused buzz of words that the other lad had opened his eyes, and after a while he saw him sit up, leaning his head upon the shoulder of one of his fellow bachelors, white and faint and sick as death.

"Thank heaven that ye did not kill him!" said Edmund Wilkes, who had been standing with the crowd looking on at the efforts of Blunt's friends to revive him, and who had now come and sat down upon the bed not far from Myles.

"Aye," said Myles, gruffly, "I do thank heaven for that."

CHAPTER · 14

IF MYLES FANCIED that one single victory over his enemy would cure the evil against which he fought, he was grievously mistaken. Wrongs are not righted so easily as that. It was only the beginning. Other and far more bitter battles lay before him before he could look around him and say, "I have won the victory."

For a day—for two days—the bachelors were demoralized at the fall of their leader, and the Knights of the Rose were proportionately uplifted.

The day that Blunt met his fall, the wooden tank in which the water had been poured every morning was found to have been taken away. The bachelors made a great show of indignation and inquiry. Who was it stole their tank? If they did but know, he should smart for it.

"Ho! ho!" roared Edmund Wilkes, so that the whole dormitory heard him. "Smoke ye not their tricks, lads? See ye not that they have stolen their own water tank, so that they might have no need for another fight over the carrying of the water?"

The bachelors made an obvious show of not having heard what he said, and a general laugh went around. No one doubted that Wilkes had spoken the truth in his taunt, and that the bachelors had indeed stolen their own tank. So no more water was ever carried for the head squires, but it was plain to see that the war for the upper hand was not yet over.

Even if Myles had entertained comforting thoughts to the contrary, he was speedily undeceived. One morning, about a week after the fight, as he and Gascoyne were crossing the armory court, they were hailed by a group of the bachelors standing at the stone steps of the great building.

"Holloa, Falworth!" they cried. "Know ye that Blunt is nigh well again?"

"Nay," said Myles; "I knew it not. But I am right glad to hear it."

"Ye'll sing a different song soon," said one of the bachelors. "I tell ye he is hot against you, and swears when he comes again he will carve ye soothly."

"Aye, marry!" said another. "I would not be in your skin a week hence for a ducat! Only this morning he told Philip Mowbray that he would have your blood for the fall ye gave him. Look to yourself, Falworth. He comes again Wednesday or Thursday next. Ye stand in a parlous state."

"Myles," said Gascoyne, as they entered the

great quadrangle, "I do indeed fear that he means to do you evil."

"I know not," said Myles, boldly; "but I fear him not." Nevertheless, his heart was heavy with the weight of impending ill.

One evening the bachelors were more than usually noisy in their end of the dormitory, laughing and talking and shouting to one another.

"Holloa, you sirrah, Falworth!" called one of them along the length of the room. "Blunt comes again tomorrow."

Myles saw Gascoyne direct a sharp glance at him, but he answered nothing either to his enemy's words or his friend's look.

As the bachelor had said, Blunt came the next morning. It was just after chapel, and the whole body of squires was gathered in the armory waiting for the orders of the day and the calling of the roll of those chosen for household duty. Myles was sitting on a bench along the wall, talking and jesting with some who stood by, when of a sudden his heart gave a great leap within him.

Walter Blunt came walking in at the door as if nothing had passed, and at his unexpected coming the hubbub of talk and laughter was suddenly checked. Even Myles stopped in his speech for a moment, and then continued with a beating heart and a carelessness of manner that was altogether assumed. In his hand Blunt carried the house orders for the day, and without seeming to notice Myles, he opened it and read the list of those called upon for household service.

Myles had risen, and was now standing listening with the others. When Blunt had ended reading the list of names, he rolled up the parchment and thrust it into his belt. Then, swinging suddenly on his heel, he strode straight up to Myles, facing him. A moment or two of deep silence followed; not a sound broke the stillness. When Blunt spoke, everyone in the armory heard his words.

"Sirrah!" said he, "ye did put foul shame upon me. Never will I forget or forgive that offence, and will have a reckoning with you right soon that ye will not forget to the last day of your life."

When Myles had seen his enemy turn upon him, he did not at first know what to expect. He would not have been surprised had they come to blows there and then, and he held himself prepared for any event. He faced the other pluckily enough and without flinching, and spoke up boldly in answer. "So be it, Walter Blunt. I fear you not in whatever way ye may encounter me."

"Do ye not?" said Blunt. "By Our Lady ye will have cause to fear me before I am through with you." He smiled a baleful, lingering smile, and then turned slowly and walked away.

"What think ye, Myles?" said Gascoyne, as the two left the armory together.

"I think naught," said Myles, gruffly. "He will not dare to touch me to harm me. I fear him not." Nevertheless, he did not speak the full feelings of his heart.

"I know not, Myles," said Gascoyne, shaking his head doubtfully. "Walter Blunt is a cunning, evil-minded knave, and I think will do whatever evil he promises."

"I fear him not," said Myles again, but his heart foreboded trouble.

The coming of the head squire made a very great change in the condition of affairs. Even before that coming the bachelors had somewhat recovered from their demoralization, and now again they began to pluck up their confidence and to order the younger squires and pages upon this personal service or upon that.

"See ye not," said Myles one day, when the Knights of the Rose were gathered in the Brutus Tower—"see ye not that they grow as bad as ever? If we do not put a stop to this overmastery now, it will never stop."

"Best let it be, Myles," said Wilkes. "They will kill you if ye cease not troubling them. Ye have bred mischief enough for yourself already."

"No matter for that," said Myles; "it is not to be borne that they order others of us about as they do. I mean to speak to them tonight, and tell them it shall not be."

He was as good as his word. That night, as the youngsters were shouting and romping and skylarking, as they always did before turning in, he stood upon his cot and shouted: "Silence! Listen!" And then, in the hush that followed—"I want those bachelors to hear this: that we squires serve them no longer, and if they would have some to wait upon them, they must get them elsewhere than here. There be twenty of us to stand against them and perhaps more, and we mean that they shall have service of us no more."

Then he jumped down from his elevated stand, and an uproar of confusion instantly filled the place. What was the effect of his words upon the bachelors he could not see. What was the result he was not slow in discovering.

The next day Myles and Gascoyne were throwing their daggers for a wager at a wooden target against the wall back of the armorer's smithy. Wilkes, Gosse, and one or two others of the squires were sitting on a bench looking on, and now and then applauding a more than usually well-aimed cast of the knife. Suddenly that impish little page spoken of before, Robin Ingoldsby, thrust his shock head around the corner of the smithy and said:

"Ho, Falworth! Blunt is going to serve you out today, and I myself heard him say so. He says he is going to slit your ears." And then he was gone as suddenly as he had appeared.

Myles darted after him, caught him midway in the quadrangle, and brought him back by the scruff of the neck, squalling and struggling.

"There!" said he, still panting from the chase, and seating the boy by no means gently upon the bench beside Wilkes. "Sit ye there, ye imp of evil! And now tell me what ye did mean by your words. If ye stop not your outcry, I will cut your throat," and he made a ferocious gesture with his dagger.

It was by no means easy to worm the story from the mischievous little monkey. He knew Myles too well to be in the least afraid of his threats. But at last, by dint of bribing and coaxing, Myles and his friends managed to get at the facts. The youngster had been sent to clean the riding boots of one of the bachelors, instead of which he had lolled idly on a cot in the dormitory, until he had at last fallen asleep. He had been awakened by the opening of the dormitory door and by the sound of voices—among them was that of his taskmaster. Fearing punishment for his neglected duty, he had slipped out of the cot and hidden himself beneath it.

Those who had entered were Walter Blunt and three of the older bachelors. Blunt's companions were trying to persuade him against something, but without avail. It was—Myles' heart thrilled and his blood boiled—to lie in wait for him, to overpower him by numbers, and to mutilate him by slitting his ears—a disgraceful punishment administered, as a rule, only for thieving and poaching.

"He would not dare to do such a thing!" cried Myles, with heaving breast and flashing eyes.

"Aye, but he would," said Gascoyne. "His father, Lord Reginald Blunt, is a great man over Nottingham way, and my lord would not dare to punish him even for such a matter as that. But tell me, Robin Ingoldsby, do you know aught more of this matter? Prithee tell it me, Robin. Where do they propose to lie in wait for Falworth?"

"In the gateway to the Buttery Court, so as to catch him when he passes by to the armory," answered the boy.

"Are they there now?" said Wilkes.

"Aye, nine of them," said Robin. "I heard Blunt tell Mowbray to go and gather the others.

He heard you tell Gosse, Falworth, that ye were going thither for your arbalest this morning to shoot at the rooks."

"That will do, Robin," said Myles. "Ye may go."

And therewith the little imp scurried off, pulling the lobes of his ears suggestively as he darted around the corner.

The others looked at one another for a while in silence.

"So, comrades," said Myles at last, "what shall we do now?"

"Go, and tell Sir James," said Gascoyne, promptly.

"Nay," said Myles, "I take no such coward's part as that. I say if they hunger to fight, give them their stomach full."

The others were very reluctant for such extreme measures, but Myles, as usual, carried his way, and so a pitched battle was decided upon. It was Gascoyne who suggested the plan which they afterward followed.

Then Wilkes started away to gather together those of the Knights of the Rose not upon household duty, and Myles, with the others, went to the armorsmith to have him make for them a set of knives with which to meet their enemies —knives with blades a foot long, pointed and double-edged.

The smith, leaning with his hammer upon the anvil, listened to them as they described the weapons.

"Nay, nay, Master Myles," said he, when Myles had ended by telling the use to which he intended putting them. "Ye are going all wrong in this matter. With such blades, before this battle

93

is ended, someone would be slain, and so murder done. Then the family of him who was killed would perhaps have ye cited, and mayhap it might even come to the hanging, for some of the boys have great folk behind them. Go ye to Tom Fletcher, Master Myles, and buy of him good yew staves, such as one might break a head with, and with them, if ye keep your wits, ye may hold your own against knives or short swords. I tell you, even though my trade be making of blades, rather would I have a good stout cudgel in my hand than the best dagger that ever was forged."

Myles stood thoughtful for a moment or two; then, looking up, "I think ye speak truly, Peter," said he; "and it were ill done to have blood upon our hands."

CHAPTER · 15

FROM THE LONG, NARROW, stone-paved Armory Court, and connecting it with the inner Buttery Court, ran a narrow, arched passageway, in which was a picket gate, closed at night and locked from within. It was in this arched passageway that, according to little Robin Ingoldsby's report, the bachelors were lying in wait for Myles. Gascoyne's plan was that Myles should enter the court alone, the Knights of the Rose lying ambushed behind the angle of the armory until the bachelors should show themselves.

It was not without trepidation that Myles walked alone into the court, which happened then to be silent and empty. His heart beat more quickly than it was wont, and he gripped his cudgel behind his back, looking sharply this way and that, so as not to be taken unawares by a flank movement of his enemies. Midway in the court he stopped and hesitated for a moment. Then he turned as though to enter the armory. The next moment he saw the bachelors come pouring out from the archway.

Instantly he turned and rushed back toward where his friends lay hidden, shouting, "To the rescue! To the rescue!"

"Stone him!" roared Blunt. "The villain escapes!"

He stooped and picked up a cobblestone as he spoke, flinging it after his escaping prey. It narrowly missed Myles' head. Had it struck him, there might have been no more of this story to tell.

"To the rescue! To the rescue!" shouted Myles' friends in answer, and the next moment he was surrounded by them. Then he turned, and swinging his cudgel, rushed back upon his foes.

The bachelors stopped short at the unexpected sight of the lads with their cudgels. For a moment they rallied and drew their knives. Then they turned and fled toward their former place of hiding.

One of them turned for a moment, and flung his knife at Myles with a deadly aim. But Myles, quick as a cat, ducked, and the weapon flew clattering across the stony court. Then he who had flung it turned again to flee, but in his attempt he had delayed one instant too long. Myles reached him with a long-arm stroke of his cudgel just as he entered the passageway, knocking him over like a bottle, stunned and senseless.

The next moment the picket gate was banged in their faces and the bolt shot in the staples, and the Knights of the Rose were left shouting and battering the palings with their cudgels.

By this time the uproar of fight had aroused those in the rooms and offices fronting upon the Armory Court. Heads were thrust from many of the windows with the eager interest that a fight always evokes.

"Beware!" shouted Myles. "Here they come again!" He bore back toward the entrance of the alleyway as he spoke, those behind him scattering to right and left, for the bachelors had rallied and were coming again to the attack, shouting.

They were not a moment too soon in this retreat, either, for the next instant the pickets flew open, and a volley of stones rained after the retreating Knights of the Rose. One smote Wilkes upon the head, knocking him down headlong. Another struck Myles upon his left shoulder, benumbing his arm from the fingertips to the armpit, so that he thought the limb was broken.

"Get ye behind the buttresses!" shouted those who looked down upon the fight from the windows "get ye behind the buttresses!" And in answer the lads, scattering like a newly flushed covey of partridges, fled to and crouched in the sheltering angles of masonry to escape from the flying stones.

And now followed a lull in the battle, the bachelors fearing to leave the protection of the arched passageway lest their retreat should be cut off, and the Knights of the Rose not daring to quit the shelter of the buttresses and angles of the wall lest they should be knocked down by the stones.

The bachelor whom Myles had struck down with his cudgel was sitting up rubbing the back of his head, and Wilkes had gathered his wits enough to crawl to the shelter of the nearest buttress. Myles, peeping around the corner behind which he stood, could see that the bachelors were gathered into a little group consulting together. Suddenly it broke asunder, and Blunt turned around.

"Ho, Falworth!" he cried. "Will ye hold truce while we parley with ye?"

"Aye," answered Myles.

"Will ye give me your honor that ye will hold your hands from harming us while we talk together?"

"Yea," said Myles, "I pledge you my honor."

"I accept your pledge. See! Here we throw aside our stones and lay down our knives. Lay ye by your clubs, and meet us in parley at the horse block yonder."

"So be it," said Myles, and thereupon, standing his cudgel in the angle of the wall, he stepped boldly out into the open courtyard. Those of his party came scatteringly from right and left, gathering about him; and the bachelors advanced in a body, led by the head squire.

"Now what is it ye would have, Walter Blunt?" said Myles, when both parties had met at the horse block.

"It is to say this to you, Myles Falworth," said the other. "Onetime, not long since, ye did challenge me to meet you hand to hand in the dormitory. Then ye did put a vile affront upon me, for the which I have brought on this battle today, for I knew not then that ye were going to try your peasant tricks of wrestling; and so, without guarding myself, I met you as ye did desire."

"But ye had a knife, and would have stabbed him could you have done so," said Gascoyne.

"You lie!" said Blunt. "I had no knife." And then, without giving time to answer, "Ye cannot deny that I met you then at your bidding, can ye, Falworth?"

"Nay," said Myles, "nor perhaps can ye deny it either." And at this covert reminder of his defeat Myles' followers laughed scoffingly and Blunt bit his lip.

"Ye have said it," said he. "Then, since I met you at your bidding, I dare you to meet me now at mine, and to fight this battle out between our two selves, with sword and buckler and basinet as gentlemen should, and not in a wrestling match like two country hodges."

"You are a cowardly wretch, Walter Blunt!" burst out Wilkes, who stood by with a swelling lump on his head, already as big as a walnut. "Well you know that Falworth is not match for you at broadsword play. Is he not four years younger than you, and have ye not had three times the practice in arms that he has had? I say ye are a coward to seek to fight with cutting weapons."

Blunt made no answer to Wilkes' speech, but gazed steadfastly at Myles, with a scornful smile curling the corners of his lips. Myles stood looking at the ground without once lifting his eyes, not knowing what to answer, for he was well aware that he was no match for Blunt with the broadsword.

"Ye are afraid to fight me, Myles Falworth," said Blunt tauntingly, and the bachelors gave a jeering laugh in echo.

Then Myles looked up, and I cannot say that his face was not a trifle whiter than usual. "Nay," said he, "I am not afraid, and I will fight you, Blunt."

"So be it," said Blunt. "Then let us go at it straightway in the armory yonder, for they be at dinner in the Great Hall, and just now there be no one by to stay us."

"Ye shall not fight him, Myles!" burst out Gascoyne. "He will murder you! Ye shall not fight him, I say!"

Myles turned away without answering him.

"What goes on?" called one of those who were still looking out of the windows as the crowd of boys passed beneath.

"Blunt and Falworth are going to fight it out hand to hand in the armory," answered one of the bachelors, looking up.

The brawling of the squires was a jest to all the adjoining part of the house. So the heads were withdrawn again, some laughing at the "sparring of the cockerels."

But it was no jesting matter to poor Myles.

CHAPTER · 16

I HAVE NO INTENTION to describe the fight between Myles Falworth and Walter Blunt. Fisticuffs are brutal and debasing enough, but a fight with a sharp-edged broadsword was not only brutal and debasing, but cruel and bloody as well.

From the very first of the fight Myles Falworth was palpably and obviously overmatched. After fifteen minutes had passed, Blunt stood hale and sound as at first, but poor Myles had more than one red stain of warm blood upon doublet and hose, and more than one bandage had been wrapped by Gascoyne and Wilkes about sore wounds.

He had received no serious injury as yet, for not only was his body protected by a buckler, or small oblong shield, which he carried upon his left arm, and his head by a basinet, or light helmet of steel, but perhaps, after all, Blunt was not overanxious to do him any dangerous harm. Nevertheless, there could be but one opinion as to how the fight tended, and Myles' friends were gloomy and downcast, the bachelors proportionately exultant, shouting with laughter, and taunting Myles at every unsuccessful stroke.

Once, as he drew back panting, leaning upon Gascoyne's shoulder, the faithful friend whispered, with trembling lips: "Oh, dear Myles, carry it no further. Ye hurt him not, and he will slay you before he have done with you."

Thereupon Blunt, who caught the drift of the speech, put in a word. "Ye are sore hurt, Myles Falworth," said he, "and I would do you no grievous harm. Yield you and own yourself beaten, and I will forgive you. Ye have fought a good fight, and there is no shame in yielding now."

"Never!" cried Myles, hoarsely—"never will I

yield me! Ye may slay me, Walter Blunt, and I reck not if ye do so, but never else will ye conquer me."

There was a tone of desperation in his voice that made all look serious.

"Nay," said Blunt. "I will fight you no more, Myles Falworth; ye have had enough."

"By heavens!" cried Myles, grinding his teeth, "ye shall fight me, you coward! Ye have brought this fight upon us, and either ye or I get our quittance here. Let go, Gascoyne!" he cried, shaking loose his friend's hold; "I tell you he shall fight me!"

From that moment Blunt began to lose his head. No doubt he had not thought of such a serious fight as this when he had given his challenge, and there was a savage bulldog tenacity about Myles that could not have had a somewhat demoralizing effect upon him.

A few blows were given and taken, and then Myles' friends gave a shout. Blunt drew back, and placed his hand to his shoulder. When he drew it away again it was stained with red, and another red stain grew and spread rapidly down the sleeve of his jacket. He stared at his hand for a moment with a half-dazed look, and then glanced quickly to right and left.

"I will fight no more," said he, sullenly.

"Then yield ye!" cried Myles, exultantly.

The triumphant shouts of the Knights of the Rose stung Blunt like a lash, and the battle began again. Perhaps some of the older lads were of a mind to interfere at this point—certainly some looked very serious—but before they interposed, the fight was ended.

Blunt, grinding his teeth, struck one undercut at his opponent—the same undercut that Myles had struck at Sir James Lee at the knight's bidding when he first practiced at the Devlen pels. Myles met the blow as Sir James had met that blow, and then struck in return as Sir James had struck—full and true. The basinet that Blunt wore glanced the blow partly, but not entirely. Myles felt his sword bite through the light steel cap, and Blunt dropped his own blade clattering upon the floor. It was all over in an instant, but in that instant what he saw was stamped upon Myles' mind with an indelible imprint. He saw the young man stagger backward; he saw the eyes roll upward, and a red streak shoot out from under the cap and run down across the cheek.

Blunt reeled half around, and then fell prostrate upon his face. Myles stood staring at him with the delirious turmoil of his battle dissolving rapidly into a dumb fear at that which he had done.

Once again he had won—but what a victory! "Is he dead?" he whispered to Gascoyne.

"I know not," said Gascoyne, with a very pale face. "But come away, Myles." And he led his friend out of the room.

Some little while later one of the bachelors came to the dormitory where Myles, his wounds smarting and aching and throbbing, lay stretched on his cot, and with a very serious face bade him go presently to Sir James, who had come from dinner and was then in his office.

By this time Myles knew that he had not slain his enemy, and his heart was light in spite of the coming interview. There was no one in the office but Sir James and himself, and Myles, without concealing anything, told, point by point, the whole trouble. Sir James sat looking steadily at him for a while after he had ended.

"Never," said he, presently, "did I know any one of ye squires, in all the time that I have been here, to get himself into so many broils as you, Myles Falworth. Perhaps ye sought to take this lad's life."

"Nay," said Myles, earnestly. "God forbid!"

"Nevertheless," said Sir James, "ye fetched him a main shrewd blow, and it is by good hap, and no fault of yours, that he will live to do more mischief yet. This is your second venture at him. The third time, maybe, ye will end him for good." Then, suddenly assuming his grimmest and sternest manner: "Now, sirrah, do I put a stop to this, and no more shall ye fight with edged tools. Get ye to the dormitory, and abide there a full week without coming forth. Michael shall bring you bread and water twice a day for that time. That is all the food ye shall have, and we will see if that fare will not cool your hot humors."

Myles had expected a punishment so much more severe than that which was meted to him that in the sudden relief he broke into a convulsive laugh, and then, with a hasty sweep, wiped a brimming moisture from his eyes.

Sir James looked keenly at him for a moment. "Ye are white in the face," said he. "Are you wounded very sorely?"

"Nay," said Myles, "it is not much, but I be sick in my stomach."

"Aye, aye," said Sir James; "I know that feeling well. It is thus that one always feels in coming out from a sore battle when one has suffered wounds and lost blood. If ye would keep yourself hale, keep yourself from needless fighting. Now go ye to the dormitory, and, as I said, come ye not forth again for a week. Stay, sirrah!" he added. "I will send George the barber to look to your sores. Green wounds are best drawn and salved before they grow cold."

I wonder what Myles would have thought had he known that as soon as he had left the office Sir James had gone straight to the Earl and recounted the whole matter to him, with a deal of dry gusto, and the Earl listened laughing.

"Aye," said he, when Sir James had done, "the boy has mettle, sure. Nevertheless, we must transplant this fellow Blunt to the office of gentleman-in-waiting. He must be old enough now, and if he stays in his present place, either he will do the boy harm or the boy will do him harm."

So Blunt never came again to trouble the squires' quarters, and thereafter the youngsters rendered no more service to the elders.

Myles' first great fight in life was won.

CHAPTER · 17

THE SUMMER PASSED AWAY, and the bleak fall came. Myles had long since accepted his position as one set apart from the others of his kind, and had resigned himself to the evident fact that he was never to serve in the household-in-waiting upon the Earl. I cannot say that it never troubled him, but in time there came a compensation of which I shall presently speak.

And then he had so much the more time to himself. The other lads were sometimes occupied by their household duties when sports were afoot in which they would have liked to take part. Myles was always free to enter into any matter of the kind after his daily exercise had been performed at the pels, the butts, or the tilting court.

But even though he was never called to do service in "my lord's house," he was not long in gaining a sort of secondhand knowledge of all the family: my lady, a thin, sallow, faded woman, not yet past middle age, but looking ten years older; the Lady Anne, the daughter of the house, a tall, thin, dark-eyed, dark-haired, handsome young girl of twenty or twenty-one years of age, hawk-nosed like her father, and silent, proud, and haughty, Myles heard the squires say. And also Lady Alice, the Earl of Mackworth's niece and ward, a great heiress in her own right, a strikingly pretty black-eyed girl of fourteen or fifteen.

These composed the Earl's personal family; but besides them was Lord George Beaumont, the Earl's brother, and Myles soon came to know him better than any of the chief people of the castle excepting Sir James Lee.

For since Myles' great battle in the armory Lord George had taken a laughing sort of liking to the lad, encouraging him at times to talk of his adventures and of his hopes and aspirations.

Perhaps the Earl's younger brother—who was himself somewhat a soldier of fortune, having fought in Spain, France, and Germany—felt a certain kinship in spirit with the adventurous youngster who had his unfriended way to make in the world. However that might have been, Lord George was very kind and friendly to the lad, and the willing service that Myles rendered him reconciled him not a little to the Earl's obvious neglect.

Besides these of the more immediate family of the Earl were a number of knights, ladies, and gentlemen, some of them cadets, some of them retainers, of the house of Beaumont, for the princely nobles of those days lived in state little less royal than royalty itself.

Most of the knights and gentlemen Myles soon came to know by sight, meeting them in Lord George's apartments in the south wing of the great house, and some of them, following the lead of Lord George, singled him out for friendly notice, giving him a nod or a word in passing.

Every season has its pleasures for boys, and the constant change that they bring is one of the greatest delights of boyhood's days.

All of us, as we grow older, have in our memory pictures of bygone times that are somehow more than usually vivid, the colors of some not blurring by time as others do. One of which, in remembering, always filled Myles' heart in after-

107

years with an indefinable pleasure, was the recollection of standing with others of his fellow squires in the crisp brown autumn grass of the paddock and shooting with the longbow at wild fowl, which, when the east wind was straining, flew low overhead to pitch to the lake in the forbidden precincts of the deer park beyond the brow of the hill. More than once a brace or two of these wild fowl, shot in their southward flight by the lads and cooked by fat, good-natured Mother Joan, graced the rude mess table of the squires in the long hall. Even the toughest and fishiest drake, when brought down by their arrows, had a savor that somehow the daintiest fare lacked in afteryears.

Then fall passed and winter came, bleak, cold, and dreary—not winter as we know it nowadays, with warm fires and bright lights to make the long nights sweet and cheerful with comfort, but winter with all its grimness and sternness. In the great, cold, stone-walled castles of those days the only fire and almost the only light were those from the huge blazing logs that roared and crackled in the large open stone fireplace around which the people gathered, sheltering their faces as best they could from the scorching heat, and cloaking their shoulders from the biting cold, for at the farther end of the room, where giant shadows swayed and bowed and danced, huge and black against the high walls, the white frost glistened in the moonlight on the stone floors, and the breath went up like smoke.

In those days there were no books to read, but only rude stories and jests, recited by some strolling mummer or minstrel to the listening circle, gathered around the blaze, who welcomed the coarse, gross jests, and coarser, grosser songs with roars of boisterous laughter.

Yet bleak and dreary as was the winter in those days, and cold and biting as was the frost in the cheerless, windy halls and corridors of the castle, it was not without its joys to the young lads, for then, as now, boys could find pleasure even in slushy weather, when the wet snow is fit for nothing but to make snowballs.

Thrice that bitter winter the moat was frozen over, and the lads, making themselves skates of marrow bones, which they bought from the hall cook at a groat a pair, went skimming over the smooth surface, red-cheeked and shouting.

Then at Yuletide, which was somewhat of a rude semblance to the merry Christmas season of our day, a great feast was held in the hall, and all the castle folk were fed in the presence of the Earl and the Countess. Oxen and sheep were roasted whole. Huge suet puddings, made of barley meal sweetened with honey and stuffed with plums, were boiled in great caldrons in the open courtyard. Barrels of ale and malmsey were broached, and all the folk, gentle and simple, were bidden to the feast. Afterward the minstrels danced and acted a rude play, and in the evening a miracle show was performed on a raised platform in the north hall.

For a week the castle was fed upon the remains of the good things left from the great feast, until everyone grew to loathe fine victuals, and longed for honest beef and mustard again.

Then, at last, in that constant change the winter was gone, and even the lads who had enjoyed its passing were glad when the winds blew warm once more and the grass showed green in sunny places, and the leader of the wild fowl honked, as they who in the fall had flown to the south flew, arrowlike, northward again; when the buds swelled and the leaves burst forth once more, and crocuses and then daffodils gleamed in the green grass like sparks and flames of gold.

With the spring came the outdoor sports of the season, among others that of ball—for boys were boys, and played at ball even in those faraway days—a game called trapball. In some parts of England it is still played just as it was in Myles Falworth's day, and enjoyed just as Myles and his friends enjoyed it.

So now that the sun was warm and the weather pleasant, the game of trapball was in full swing every afternoon. The playground was an open space between the wall that surrounded the castle grounds and that of the privy garden in which the ladies of the Earl's family took the air every day, and upon which their apartments opened.

Now one fine breezy afternoon, when the lads were shouting and playing at this, their favorite game, Myles himself was at the trap barehanded and barearmed. The wind was blowing from behind him, and, aided perhaps by it, he had already struck three or four balls nearly the whole length of the court—an unusual distance—and several of the lads had gone back almost to the wall of the privy garden to catch any ball that might chance to fly as far as that. Then once more Myles struck, throwing all his strength into the blow. The ball shot up into the air, and when it fell, it dropped within the privy garden.

The shouts of the young players were instantly stilled, and Gascoyne, who stood nearest Myles, thrust his hands into his belt, giving a long, shrill whistle.

"This time ye have struck us all out, Myles," said he. "There be no more play for us until we get another ball."

The outfielders came slowly trooping in until they had gathered in a little circle around Myles.

"I could not help it," said Myles, in answer to their grumbling. "How knew I the ball would fly so far? But if I have lost the ball, I can get it again. I will climb the wall for it."

"Ye shall do naught of the kind, Myles," said Gascoyne, hastily. "Ye are as mad as a March hare to think of such a venture! Would get yourself shot with a bolt betwixt the ribs, like poor Diccon Cook?"

Of all places about the castle the privy garden was perhaps the most sacred. It was a small plot of ground, only a few rods long and wide, and was kept absolutely private for the use of the Countess and her family. Only a little while before Myles had first come to Devlen, one of the cook's men had been found climbing the wall, whereupon the soldier who saw him shot him with his crossbow. The poor fellow dropped from the wall into the garden, and when they found him, he still held a bunch of flowers in his hand, which he had perhaps been gathering for his sweetheart.

Had Myles seen him carried on a litter to the infirmary as Gascoyne and some of the others had done, he might have thought twice before venturing to enter the ladies' private garden. But he only shook his stubborn head, and said again, "I will climb the wall and fetch it."

Now at the lower extremity of the court, and about twelve or fifteen feet distant from the garden wall, there grew a pear tree, some of the branches of which overhung into the garden beyond. So, first making sure that no one was looking that way, and bidding the others keep a sharp lookout, Myles shinned up this tree, and choosing one of the thicker limbs, climbed out upon it for some little distance. Then, lowering his body, he hung at arm's length, the branch bending with his weight, and slowly let himself down hand over hand, until at last he hung directly over the top of the wall and perhaps a foot above it. Below him he could see the leafy top of an arbor covered with a thick growth of clematis, and even as he hung there he noticed the broad, smooth walks, the grassy terrace in front of the Countess' apartments in the distance, the quaint flower beds, the yew trees trimmed into odd shapes, and even the deaf old gardener working barearmed in the sunlight at a flower bed in the far corner by the toolhouse.

The top of the wall was pointed like a house roof, and immediately below him was covered by a thick growth of green moss. It flashed through his mind as he hung there that maybe it would offer a very slippery foothold for one dropping upon the steep slopes of the top. But it was too late to draw back now.

Bracing himself for a moment, he loosed his hold upon the limb above. The branch flew back with a rush, and he dropped, striving to grasp the sloping angle with his feet. Instantly the teacherous, slippery moss slid away from beneath him. He made a vain clutch at the wall, his fingers sliding over the cold stones; then, with a sharp exclamation, down he pitched bodily into the garden beneath. A thousand thoughts flew through his brain like a cloud of flies, and then a leafy greenness seemed to strike up against him. A splintering crash sounded in his ears as the lattice top of the arbor broke under him, and with one final clutch at the empty air he fell heavily upon the ground beneath.

He heard a shrill scream that seemed to find an instant echo. Even as he fell he had a vision of faces and bright colors, and when he sat up, dazed and bewildered, he found himself face to face with the Lady Anne, the daughter of the house, and her cousin, the Lady Alice, who, clutching each other tightly, stood staring at him with wide, scared eyes.

CHAPTER · 18

FOR A LITTLE TIME there was deep silence, during which the fluttering leaves came drifting down from the broken arbor above.

It was the Lady Anne who spoke first. "Who are you, and whence do you come?" said she, tremulously.

Then Myles gathered himself up sheepishly. "My name is Myles Falworth," said he, "and I am one of the squires of the body."

"Oh! aye!" said the Lady Alice, suddenly. "I thought I knew your face. Are ye not the young man that I have seen in Lord George's service?"

"Yes, lady," said Myles, twining a piece of the broken vine in and out among his fingers. "Lord George has often had me of late about his person."

"And what do ye here, sirrah?" said the Lady Anne, angrily. "How dare ye come so into our garden?"

"I meant not to come as I did," said Myles, clumsily, and with a face hot and red, "but I slipped over the top of the wall and fell hastily into the garden. Truly, lady, I meant ye no harm or fright thereby."

He looked so drolly abashed as he stood before them, with his clothes torn and soiled from the fall, his face red, and his eyes downcast, all the while industriously twisting the piece of clematis in and around his fingers, that the Lady Anne's half-frightened anger could not last. She

114

and her cousin exchanged glances, and smiled at each other.

"But," said she at last, trying to draw her pretty brows together into a frown, "tell me: why did ye seek to climb the wall?"

"I came to seek a ball," said Myles, "which I struck over hither from the court beyond."

"And would ye come into our privy garden for no better reason than to find a ball?" said the young lady.

"Nay," said Myles; "it was not so much to find the ball, but, in good sooth, I did truly strike it harder than need be, and so, when I lost the ball, I could do no less than come and find it again, else our sport is done for the day. So it was I came hither."

The two young ladies had by now recovered from their fright. The Lady Anne slyly nudged her cousin with her elbow, and the younger could not suppress a half-nervous laugh. Myles heard it, and felt his face grow hotter and redder than ever.

"Nay," said the Lady Anne, "I do believe Master Giles—"

"My name is Myles," corrected Myles.

"Very well then, Master Myles. I say I do believe that ye mean no harm in coming hither. Nevertheless it was ill of you to do so. If my father should find you here, he would have you severely punished for such trespassing. Do ye not know that no one is permitted to enter this place? No, not even my Uncle George. One fellow who came hither to steal apples once had his ears shaven close to his head, and not more than a year ago one of the cook's men who climbed the wall early one morning was shot by the watchman."

"Aye," said Myles, "I knew of him who was shot, and it did go somewhat against my stomach to venture, knowing what had happened to him. Nevertheless, if I did not get the ball, how were we to play more today at the trap?"

"Marry, you are a bold fellow, I do believe me," said the young lady, "and since ye have come in the face of such peril to get your ball, ye shall not go away empty. Whither did ye strike it?"

"Over yonder by the pear tree," said Myles, jerking his head in that direction. "If I may go get it, I will trouble ye no more." As he spoke he made a motion to leave them.

"Stay!" said the Lady Anne, hastily; "remain where you are. If ye cross the open space, someone perhaps may see you from the house, and will give the alarm, and ye will be lost. I will go get your ball."

And so she left Myles and her cousin, crossing the little plots of grass and skirting the rose bushes to the pear tree.

When Myles found himself alone with the Lady Alice, he knew not where to look or what to do, but twisted the piece of clematis which he still held in and out more industriously than ever.

The Lady Alice watched him with dancing eyes for a little while. "Maybe ye will spoil that poor vine," said she by and by, breaking the silence and laughing, then turning serious again, "Did ye hurt yourself by your fall?"

"Nay," said Myles, looking up; "such a fall as

that was no great matter. Many and many a time I have had worse."

"Have you?" said the Lady Alice. "Ye did frighten me greatly, and my cousin likewise."

Myles hesitated for a moment, and then blurted out, "Thereat I grieve, for you I would not frighten for all the world."

The young lady laughed and blushed. "All the world is a great matter," said she.

"Yea," said he, "it is a great matter. But it is a greater matter to frighten you, and so I would not do it for that, and more."

The young lady laughed again, but she did not say anything further. By and by she forced herself to say, "My cousin finds not the ball."

"Nay," said Myles, briefly, and then again neither spoke, until the Lady Anne came, bringing the ball. Myles felt a great sense of relief at her coming, and yet was somehow sorry. Then he took the ball, and knew enough to bow his acknowledgment in a manner neither ill nor awkward.

"Did ye hurt yourself?" said the Lady Anne.

"Nay," said Myles, giving himself a shake; "see ye not I am whole, limb and bone? Nay, I have had worse falls than that. Once I fell out of an oak tree down by the river and upon a root, and broke a rib or more. And then one time when I was a boy in Crosbey-Dale—that was where I lived before I came hither—I did catch hold of the blade of the windmill, thinking it was moving slowly, and that I would have a ride in the air, and so was like to have had a fall ten thousand times worse than this."

"Oh, tell us more of that!" said the Lady Anne,

eagerly. "I never heard of such an adventure as that. Come, cousin, and sit down here upon the bench, and let us have him tell us all of that happening."

Now the lads upon the other side of the wall had been whistling furtively for some time, not knowing whether Myles had broken his neck or had come off scot-free from his fall. "I would like right well to stay with ye," said he, irresolutely, "and would gladly tell ye that and more if ye would have me to do so, but hear ye not my friends call me from beyond? Maybe they think I broke my back, and are calling to see whether I be alive or no. If I might whistle them answer and toss this ball to them, all would then be well, and they would know that I was not hurt, and so perchance, would go away."

"Then answer them," said the Lady Anne, "and tell us of that thing ye spoke of—how ye took a ride on the windmill. We young ladies do hear little of such matters, not being allowed to talk with lads. All that we hear of perils are of knights and ladies and jousting, and such like. It would pleasure us right well to have you tell of your adventures."

So Myles tossed back the ball, and whistled in answer to his friends.

Then he told the two young ladies not only of his adventure on the windmill, but also of other boyish escapades, and told them well, with a straightforward smack and vigor, for he enjoyed adventure and loved to talk of it. In a little while he had regained his ease. His shyness and awkwardness left him, and nothing remained but the delightful fact that he was really and actually talking to two young ladies, and that with just as much ease and infinitely more pleasure than could be had in discourse with his fellow squires. But at last it was time for him to go. "Marry," said he, with a half-sigh, "I think I did never have so sweet and pleasant a time in all my life before. Never did I know a real lady to talk with, saving only my mother, and I do tell ye plain I would rather talk with ye than with any man in Christendom —saving, perhaps, only my friend Gascoyne. I would I might come hither again."

The honest frankness of his speech was irresistible. The two girls exchanged glances and then began laughing. "Truly," said the Lady Anne, who, as was said before, was some three or four years older than Myles, "ye are a bold lad to ask such a thing. How would ye come hither? Would ye tumble through our clematis arbor again, as ye did this day?"

"Nay," said Myles, "I would not do that again, but if ye will bid me do so, I will find the means to come hither."

"Nay," said the Lady Anne. "I dare not bid ye do such a foolhardy thing. Nevertheless, if ye have the courage to come—"

"Yea," said Myles, eagerly, "I have the courage."

"Then, if ye have, we will be here in the garden on Saturday next at this hour. I would like right well to hear more of your adventures. But what did ye say was your name? I have forgot it again."

"It is Myles Falworth."

"Then we shall call you Sir Myles, for you are a truly knight-errant. And stay! Every knight must have a lady to serve. How would you like my Cousin Alice for your true lady?"

"Aye," said Myles, eagerly, "I would like it right well." And then he blushed fiery red at his boldness.

"I want no knight-errant to serve me," said the Lady Alice, blushing, in answer. "Ye do ill to tease me, cousin! If ye are so free in choosing him a lady to serve, ye may choose him yourself for your pains."

"Nay," said the Lady Anne, laughing. "I say ye shall be his true lady, and he shall be your true knight. Who knows? Perchance he may serve you in some wondrous adventure, like as Chaucer tells of. But now, Sir Knight-Errant, ye must take your leave of us, and I must even let you privily out by the postern wicket. And if ye will take the risk upon you and come hither again, prithee be wary in that coming, lest in venturing ye have your ears clipped in most unknightly fashion."

That evening, as he and Gascoyne sat together on a bench under the trees in the great quadrangle, Myles told of his adventure of the afternoon, and his friend listened with breathless interest.

"But, Myles," cried Gascoyne, "did the Lady Anne never once seem proud and unkind?"

"Nay," said Myles; "only at first, when she chid me for falling through the roof of their arbor. And to think, Francis! The Lady Anne herself bade me hold the Lady Alice as my true lady, and to serve her in all knightliness!" Then he told his friend that he was going to the privy garden again on the next Saturday, and that the Lady Anne had given him permission so to do.

Gascoyne gave a long, wondering whistle, and then sat quite still, staring into the sky. By and by he turned to his friend and said, "I give you my pledge, Myles Falworth, that never in all my life did I hear of anyone that had such marvelous strange happenings befall him as ye."

Whenever the opportunity occurred for sending a letter to Crosbey-Dale, Myles wrote one to his mother; and one can guess how they were treasured by the good lady, and read over and over again to the blind old lord as he sat staring into the darkness with his sightless eyes.

About the time of this escapade he wrote a letter telling of those doings, wherein, after speaking of his misadventure of falling from the wall, and of his acquaintance with the young ladies, he went on to speak of the manner in which he repeated his visits. The letter was worded in the English of that day—the quaint and crabbed language in which Chaucer wrote. Perhaps few boys could read it nowadays, so, modernizing it somewhat, it ran thus:

"And now to let ye know that thing that followed that happening that made me acquainted with the two young damoiselles. I take me to the south wall of that garden one day four and twenty great spikes, which Peter Smith did forge for me, and for which I pay him fivepence, and that all the money that I had left of my half-year's wage, and do not know where I may get more at these present, withouten I do betake me to Sir James, who, as I did tell ye, hath consented to hold those moneys that Prior Edward gave me till I need them.

"Now these same spikes, I say, I take me them down behind the corner of the wall, and there drave them betwixt the stones, my very dear comrade and true friend Gascoyne helping me thereto to do. And so come Saturday, I climb over the wall and to the roof of the toolhouse below, seeking a fitting opportunity when I might so do without being in too great jeopardy.

"Yea; and who should be there but they two ladies, biding my coming, who, seeing me, made as though they had expected me not, and gave me greatest rebuke for adventuring so moughtily. Yet methinks were they right well pleasured that I should so adventure, which indeed I might not otherwise do, seeing, as I have telled to you, that one of them is mine own true lady for to serven, and so was the only way that I might come to speech with her."

Such was Myles' own quaint way of telling how he accomplished his aim of visiting the forbidden garden, and no doubt the smack of adventure and the savor of danger in the undertaking recommended him not a little to the favor of the young ladies.

After this first acquaintance perhaps a month passed, during which Myles had climbed the wall some half-a-dozen times (for the Lady Anne would not permit too frequent visits), and during which the first acquaintance of the three ripened rapidly to an honest, pleasant friendship. More than once Myles, when in attendance on Lord George, caught a covert smile or half-nod from one or both of the girls, not a little delightful in its very secret friendliness.

CHAPTER · 19

As was said, perhaps a month passed; then Myles' visits came to an abrupt termination, and with it ended, in a certain sense, a chapter of his life.

One Saturday afternoon he climbed the garden wall, and skirting behind a long row of rosebushes that screened him from the Countess' terrace, came to a little summerhouse where the two young ladies had appointed to meet him that day.

A pleasant half-hour or so was passed, and then it was time for Myles to go. He lingered for a while before he took his final leave, leaning against the doorpost and laughingly telling how he and some of his brother squires had made a figure of straw dressed in men's clothes, and had played a trick with it one night upon a watchman against whom they bore a grudge.

The young ladies were listening with laughing faces when suddenly Myles saw the smile vanish from the Lady Alice's eyes and a wide terror take its place. She gave a half-articulate cry, and rose abruptly from the bench upon which she was sitting.

Myles turned sharply, and then his very heart seemed to stand still within him, for there, standing in the broad sunlight, and glaring in upon the party with baleful eyes, was the Earl of Mackworth himself.

How long was the breathless silence that followed Myles never could tell. He knew that the Lady Anne had also risen, and that she and her cousin were standing as still as statues. Presently the Earl pointed to the house with his staff, and Myles noted how it trembled in his hand.

"Ye wenches," said he at last, in a hard, harsh voice—"ye wenches, what means this? Would ye deceive me so, and hold parlance thus secretly with this fellow? I will settle with him later. Meantime, get ye straightway to the house and to your rooms, and there abide until I give ye leave to come forth again. Go, I say!"

"Father," said the Lady Anne, in a breathless voice—she was as white as death, and moistened her lips with her tongue before she spoke—"Father, ye will not do harm to this young man. Spare him, I do beseech you, for truly it was I who bade him come hither. I know that he would not have come but at our bidding."

The Earl stamped his foot upon the gravel. "Did ye not hear me?" said he, still pointing to the house with his trembling staff. "I bade ye go to your rooms. I will settle with this fellow, I say, as I deem fitting."

"Father," began the Lady Anne again. But the Earl made such a savage gesture that the poor Lady Alice uttered a faint shriek, and the Lady Anne stopped abruptly, trembling. Then she turned and passed out the farther door of the summerhouse, the poor little Lady Alice following, holding her tightly by the skirts, and trembling and shuddering as though with a fit of the ague.

The Earl stood looking grimly after them from under his shaggy eyebrows, until they passed away behind the yew trees, appeared again upon the terrace behind, entered the open doors of the women's house, and were gone. Myles heard their footsteps growing fainter and fainter, but he never raised his eyes. Upon the ground at his feet were four pebbles, and he noticed how they almost made a square, and would do so if he pushed one of them with his toe, and then it seemed strange to him that he should think of such a foolish little thing at that dreadful time.

He knew that the Earl was looking gloomily at him, and that his face must be very pale. Suddenly Lord Mackworth spoke. "What have ye to say?" said he, harshly.

Then Myles raised his eyes, and the Earl smiled grimly as he looked his victim over. "I have naught to say," said the lad, huskily.

"Did ye not hear what my daughter said?"

asked the Earl. "She said that ye came not of your own free will. What say ye to that, sirrah? Is it true?"

Myles hesitated for a moment or two. His throat was tight and dry.

"Nay," said he at last, "she lies. It was I who first came into the garden. I fell by chance from the tree yonder—I was seeking a ball—then I asked those two if I might not come hither again, and so have done some several times in all. But as for her—nay, it was not at her bidding that I came, but by my own asking."

The Earl gave a little grunt. "And how often have ye been here?" said he, presently.

Myles thought a moment or two. "This makes the seventh time," said he.

Another silence followed, and Myles began to pluck up some heart that maybe all would yet be well. The Earl's next speech dashed that hope into a thousand fragments. "Well ye know," said he, "that it is forbidden for any to come here. Well ye know that twice have men been punished for this thing that ye have done, and yet ye came in spite of all. Now do ye know what ye will suffer?"

Myles picked with nervous fingers at a crack in the oaken post against which he leaned. "Maybe ye will kill me," said he at last, in a dull, choking voice.

Again the Earl smiled a grim smile. "Nay," said he, "I would not slay you, for ye have gentle blood. But what say ye should I shear your ears from your head, or perchance have you scourged in the great court?"

The sting of the words sent the blood flying

back to Myles' face again, and he looked up quickly. "Nay," said he, with a boldness that surprised himself; "Ye shall do no such unlordly thing upon me as that. I be your peer, sir, in blood; and though ye may kill me, ye have no right to shame me!"

Lord Mackworth bowed with a mocking courtesy. "Marry!" said he. "I thought it was one of my own saucy popinjay squires that I caught sneaking here and talking to those two foolish young lasses, and, lo! it is a young lord—or mayhap ye are a young prince—and commands me that I shall not do this and I shall not do that. I crave your lordship's honorable pardon, if I have said aught that may have galled you."

The fear Myles had felt was now beginning to dissolve in rising wrath. "Nay," said he, stoutly, "I be no lord and I be no prince, but I be as good as ye. For am I not the son of your onetime very true comrade and your kinsman—to wit, the Lord Falworth, who, as ye know, is poor and broken, and blind and helpless, and outlawed and banned! Yet," cried he, grinding his teeth, as the thought of it all rushed in upon him, "I would rather be in his place than in yours. For though he be ruined, you—"

He had just sense enough to stop there.

The Earl, gripping his staff behind his back, and with his head a little bent, was looking keenly at the lad from under his shaggy gray brows. "Well," said he, as Myles stopped, "ye have gone too far now to draw back. Say your say to the end. Why would ye rather be in your father's stead than in mine?"

Myles did not answer.

"Ye shall finish your speech, or else show yourself a coward. Though your father is ruined, ye did say I am—what?"

Myles keyed himself up to the effort, and then blurted out, "ye are attainted with shame."

A long, breathless silence followed.

"Myles Falworth," said the Earl at last (and even in the whirling of his wits Myles wondered that he had the name so pat)—"Myles Falworth, of all the bold, mad, harebrained fools, ye are the most foolish. How do ye dare say such words to me? Do ye not know that ye make your coming punishment ten times more bitter by such a speech?"

"Aye!" cried Myles, desperately. "But what else could I do? If I did not say the words, ye would call me coward, and coward I am not."

"By Our Lady!" said the Earl, "I do believe you. Ye are as bold and impudent a varlet as ever lived—to beard me so. Hark; ye say I think naught of my old comrade. I will show you that ye do belie me. I will suffer what ye have said to me for his sake, and for his sake will forgive you your coming hither—which I would not do in another case to any other man. Now get you gone straightway, and come hither no more. Yonder is the postern gate. Mayhap ye know the way. But stay! How came ye hither?"

Myles told him of the spikes he had driven in the wall, and the Earl listened, stroking his beard. When the lad had ended, he fixed a sharp look upon him. "But ye drove not those spikes alone," said he. "Who helped you do it?"

"That I may not tell," said Myles, firmly.

"So be it," said the Earl. "I will not ask you to tell his name. Now get ye gone! And as for those spikes, knock them out of the wall, since ye drove them in. Play no more pranks if ye would keep your skin whole. And now go, I say!"

Myles needed no further bidding, but turned and left the Earl without another word. As he went out the postern gate he looked over his shoulder. The tall figure, in its long, fur-trimmed gown, was still standing in the middle of the path, looking after him from under the shaggy eyebrows.

As he ran across the quadrangle, his heart still fluttering in his breast, he muttered to himself, "The old grizzle-beard. If I had not faced him a bold front, mayhap he would have put such shame upon me as he said. I wonder why he stood staring after me as I left the garden."

Then for the time the matter slipped from his mind, except that part that smacked of adventure.

CHAPTER · 20

So FOR A LITTLE WHILE Myles was disposed to
congratulate himself upon having come off so well
from his adventure with the Earl. But after a
day or two had passed, and he had had time
for second thought, he began to doubt whether,
after all, he might not have carried it with a
better air if he had shown more chivalrous boldness in the presence of his true lady; whether it
would not have redounded more to his credit if
he had in some way asserted his rights as the
young lady's knight-errant and defender. Was
it not ignominious to resign his rights and priv-
ileges so easily and tamely at a signal from the
Earl?

"For, in truth," said he to Gascoyne, as the
two talked the matter over, "she has, in a certain way, accepted me for her knight, and yet I
stood there without saying so much as one single word in her behalf."

"Nay," said Gascoyne, "I would not be troubled on that score. I think that ye did come off wondrous well out of the business. I would not have thought it possible that my lord could have been so patient with you as he showed himself. He must hold you in high esteem."

"Truly," said Myles, after a pause of meditative silence, "I know not of any esteem, yet I do think he was passing patient with me in this matter. But nevertheless, Francis, that does not change my stand in the case. Yea, I did shamefully, so to resign my lady without speaking one word; nor will I so resign her even yet. I have thought much of this matter of late, Francis, and now I come to you to help me. I would have ye act the part of a true friend to me—like that one I have told you of in the story of the Emperor Justinian. I would have ye, when next ye serve in the house, so to contrive that my Lady Alice shall get a letter which I shall presently write, and wherein I may set all that is crooked straight again."

"Heaven forbid," said Gascoyne, hastily, "that I should be such a fool as to burn my fingers in drawing your chestnuts from the fire! Deliver the letter yourself, good fellow!"

So spoke Gascoyne, yet after all he ended, as he usually did, by yielding to Myles' superior will and persistence. So the letter was written, and one day the good-natured Gascoyne carried it with him to the house, and the opportunity offering, gave it to one of the young ladies attendant upon the Countess' family—a lass with whom he was friendly—to be delivered to the Lady Alice.

But if Myles congratulated himself upon the success of this new adventure, it was not for long. That night, as the crowd of pages and squires were making themselves ready for bed, the call came through the uproar for "Myles Falworth! Myles Falworth!"

"Here am I," cried Myles, standing up on his cot. "Who calls me?"

It was the groom of the Earl's bedchamber. Seeing Myles standing thus raised above the others, he came walking down the length of the room toward him, the wonted hubbub gradually subsiding as he advanced, and the youngsters turning, staring, and wondering.

"My lord would speak with you, Myles Falworth," said the groom, when he had come close enough to where Myles stood. "Hurry and make ready. He is at livery even now."

The groom's words fell upon Myles like a blow. He stood for a while staring wide-eyed. "My lord speak with me!" he ejaculated at last.

"Aye," said the other, impatiently; "get you ready quickly. I must return."

Myles' head was in a whirl as he hastily changed his clothes for a better suit, Gascoyne helping him. What could the Earl want with him at this hour? He knew in his heart what it was. The interview could concern nothing but the letter that he had sent to the Lady Alice that day. As he followed the groom through the now dark and silent courts, and across the corner of the great quadrangle, and so to the Earl's house, he tried to brace his failing courage to meet the coming interview. Nevertheless, his heart beat tumultuously as he followed the other down the long corridor, lit only by a flaring torch set in a wrought-iron bracket. Then his conductor lifted the hanging at the door of the bedchamber, whence came the murmuring sound of many voices, and, holding it aside, beckoned him to enter. Myles passed within. At first he was conscious of nothing but a crowd of people and of the brightness of many lighted candles. Then he saw that he stood in a great airy room spread with the mat of woven rushes. On three sides the walls were hung with tapestry representing hunting and battle scenes. At the farther end, where the bed stood, the stone wall of the fourth side was covered with cloth of blue, embroidered with silver goshawks. Even now, in the warm springtime of May, the room was still chilly, and a great fire roared and crackled in the huge gaping mouth of the stone fireplace. Not far from the blaze were clustered the greater part of those present, buzzing in talk, now and then swelled by murmuring laughter. Some of those who knew Myles nodded to him, and two or three spoke to him as he stood waiting, while the groom went forward to speak to the Earl; though what they said and what he answered, Myles, in his bewilderment and fear, hardly knew.

As was said before, the livery was the last meal of the day, and was taken in bed. It was a simple repast—a small loaf of bread of pure white flour, a loaf of household bread, sometimes a lump of cheese, and either a great flagon of ale or of sweet wine, warm and spiced. The Earl was sitting upright in bed, dressed in a furred dressing gown, and propped up by two cylindrical bolsters of crimson satin. Upon the coverlet, and spread over his knees, was a large white napkin of linen fringed with silver thread, and on it rested a silver tray containing the bread and some cheese. Two pages and three gentlemen were waiting upon him, and Mad Noll, the jester, stood at the head of the bed, now and then jingling his bauble and passing some quaint jest on the chance of making his master smile. On a table nearby were some dozen or so wax tapers stuck on as many spiked candlesticks of silver gilt, and illuminating that end of the room with their bright, twinkling flames. One of the gentlemen was in the act of serving the Earl with a goblet of wine, poured from a silver ewer by one of the squires, as the groom of the chamber came forward and spoke. The Earl, taking the goblet, turned his head, and as Myles looked, their eyes met. Then the Earl turned away again and raised the cup to his lips, while Myles felt his heart beat more rapidly than ever.

But at last the meal was ended, and the Earl washed his hands and his mouth and his beard from a silver basin of scented water held by one of the squires. Then, leaning back against the pillows, he beckoned to Myles.

In answer Myles walked forward the length of the room, conscious that all eyes were fixed upon him. The Earl said something, and those who stood near drew back as Myles came forward. Then Myles found himself standing beside the bed, looking down upon the quilted counterpane, feeling that the other was gazing fixedly at him.

"I sent for you," said the Earl at last, still looking steadily at him, "because this afternoon there came a letter to my hand which ye had written to my niece, the Lady Alice. I have it here," said he, thrusting his hand under the bolster, "and have just now finished reading it." Then, after a moment's pause, while he opened the parchment and scanned it again, "I find no matter of harm in it, but hereafter write no more such." He spoke entirely without anger, and Myles looked up in wonder. "Here, take it," said the Earl, folding the letter and tossing it to Myles, who instinctively caught it, "and henceforth trouble ye my niece no more either by letter or any other way. I thought ye would be at some such saucy trick, and I made Alice promise to let me know when it happened. Now, I say, let this be an end of the matter. Do ye not know ye may injure her by such witless folly as that of meeting her privily and privily writing to her?"

"I meant no harm," said Myles.

"I believe you," said the Earl. "That will do now. Ye may go."

Myles hesitated.

"What would ye say?" said Lord Mackworth.

"Only this," said Myles, "if I have your leave so to do, that the Lady Alice has chosen me to be her knight, and so, whether I may see her or speak with her or no, the laws of chivalry give me, who am gentle born, the right to serve her as a true knight may."

"As a true fool may," said the Earl, dryly. "Why ye are not a knight yet, nor anything but a raw

135

lump of a boy. What rights do the laws of chivalry give you, sirrah? Ye are a fool!"

Had the Earl been ever so angry, his words would have been less bitter to Myles than his cool, unmoved patience. It mortified his pride and galled it to the quick.

"I know that ye do hold me in contempt," he mumbled.

"Out upon you!" said the Earl, testily. "Ye do tease me beyond patience. I hold you in contempt, forsooth! Why, look you, had ye been other than ye are, I would have had you whipped out of my house long since. Think ye I would have borne so patiently with another one of the squires had such a one held secret meeting with my daughter and niece, and tampered, as ye have done, with my household, sending through one of my people that letter? You are a fool, Myles Falworth!"

Myles stood staring at the Earl without making an effort to speak. The words that he had heard suddenly flashed, as it were, a new light into his mind. In that flash he fully recognized, and for the first time, the strange and wonderful forbearance the great Earl had shown to him, a poor obscure boy. What did it mean? Was Lord Mackworth his secret friend after all, as Gascoyne had more than once asserted? So Myles stood silent, thinking many things.

Meantime the other lay back upon the cylindrical bolsters, looking thoughtfully at him. "How old are ye?" said he at last.

"Seventeen last April," answered Myles.

"Then ye are old enough to have some of the thoughts of a man, and to lay aside those of a boy. Perhaps ye have had foolish things in your head this short time past. It is time that ye put them away. Harkee, sirrah! The Lady Alice is a great heiress in her own right, and may command the best alliance in England—an earl—a duke. She grows apace to a woman, and then her kind will be found in courts and great houses. As for you, ye are but a poor lad, penniless and without friends to aid you to open advancement. Your father is attainted, and one whisper of where he lies hid would bring him thence to the Tower, and perhaps to the block. Besides that, he has an enemy, as Sir James Lee has already told you—an enemy perhaps more great and powerful than myself. That enemy watches for your father and for you. Should ye dare raise your head or your fortune ever so little, he would crop them both, and that exceedingly quickly. Myles Falworth, how do ye dare to lift your eyes to the Lady Alice de Mowbray?"

Poor Myles stood silent and motionless. "Sir," said he at last, in a dry, choking voice, "ye are right, and I have been a fool. Sir, I will never raise my eyes to look upon the Lady Alice more."

"I say not that either, boy," said the Earl. "But before ye do so dare, ye must first place yourself and your family whence ye fell. Till then, as ye are an honest man, trouble her not. Now get ye gone."

As Myles crossed the dark and silent courtyard and looked up at the clear, still twinkle of the stars, he felt a kind of dull wonder that they and the night and the world should seem so much the same and he be so different.

The first stroke had been given that was to break in pieces his boyhood life. The second was soon to follow.

CHAPTER · 21

Now and then there are times in the life of everyone when new and strange things occur with such rapidity that one has hardly time to catch one's breath between the happenings. It is as though the old were crumbling away—breaking in pieces—to give place to the new that is soon to take its place.

So it was with Myles Falworth about this time. The very next day after this interview in the bedchamber, word came to him that Sir James Lee wished to speak with him in the office. He found the lean, grizzled old knight alone, sitting at the heavy oaken table with a tankard of spiced ale at his elbow and a dish of wafers and some fragments of cheese on a pewter platter before him. He pointed to his clerk's seat—a joint stool somewhat like a camp chair, but made of heavy oaken braces and with a seat of hogskin—and bade Myles be seated.

It was the first time that Myles had ever heard of such courtesy being extended to one of the company of squires, and, much wondering, he obeyed the invitation, or rather command, and sat down.

The old knight regarded him for a while in silence, his one eye, as bright and as steady as that of a hawk, looking keenly from under the penthouse of its bushy brows, while he slowly twirled and twisted his bristling, wiry mustaches, as was his custom when in meditation. At last he broke the silence. "How old are ye?" said he, abruptly.

"I turned seventeen last April," Myles answered, as he had the evening before to Lord Mackworth.

"Humph!" said Sir James. "Ye be big of bone and frame for your age. I would that your heart were more that of a man likewise and less that of a giddy, harebrained boy, thinking continually of naught but mischief."

Again he fell silent, and Myles sat quite still, wondering if it was because of any special one of his latest escapades that he had been summoned to the office—the breaking of the window in the Long Hall by the stone he had flung at the rook, or the climbing of the South Tower for the jackdaw's nest.

"Ye have a friend," said Sir James, suddenly breaking into his speculations, "of such a kind that few in this world possess. Almost ever since ye have been here he has been watching over you. Can ye guess of whom I speak?"

"Perhaps it is Lord George Beaumont," said Myles. "He has always been passing kind to me."

"Nay," said Sir James, "it is not of him that I speak, though he likes you well enough. Can ye keep a secret, boy?" he asked, suddenly.

"Yea," answered Myles.

"And will ye do so in this case if I tell you who it is that is your best friend here?"

"Yea."

"Then it is my lord who is that friend—the Earl himself. But see that ye breathe not a word of it."

Myles sat staring at the old knight in utter and profound amazement. Presently Sir James continued:

"Yea, almost ever since ye came here my lord has kept oversight of all your doings, of all your mad pranks, and your quarrels and fights, your goings out and comings in. What do ye think of that, Myles Falworth?"

Again the old knight stopped and regarded the lad, who sat silent, finding no words to answer. He seemed to take a grim pleasure in the youngster's bewilderment and wonder. Then a sudden thought came to Myles.

"Sir," said he, "did my lord know that I went to the privy garden as I did?"

"Nay," said Sir James; "of that he knew naught at first until your father bade your mother write and tell him."

"My father!" ejaculated Myles.

"Aye," said Sir James, twisting his mustaches more vigorously than ever. "As soon as your father heard of that prank, he wrote straightway to my lord that he should put a stop to what might in time have bred mischief."

"Sir," said Myles, in an almost breathless voice, "I know not how to believe all these things, or whether I be awake or adreaming."

"Ye be surely enough awake," answered the old man. "But there are other matters yet to be told. My lord thinks, as others of us do—Lord George and myself—that it is now time for you to put away your boyish follies, and learn those things

140

pertaining to manhood. Ye have been here a year now, and have had freedom to do as ye might list, but boy"—and the old warrior spoke seriously, almost solemnly—"upon you do rest matters of such great import that did I tell them to you ye could not grasp them. My lord deems that ye have, perhaps, promise beyond the common of men. Nevertheless it remains yet to be seen if he be right. It is yet to test whether that promise may be fulfilled. Next Monday I and Sir Everard Willoughby take you in hand to begin training you in the knowledge and the use of the jousting lance, of arms, and of horsemanship. Ye are to go to Peter Smith, and have him fit a suit of plain armor to you which he has been charged to make for you. So get you gone, think well over all these matters, and prepare yourself by next Monday. But stay, sirrah," he added, as Myles, dazed and bewildered, turned to obey. "Breathe to no living soul what I have told you—that my lord is your friend—neither speak of anything concerning him. Such is his own heavy command laid upon you."

Then Myles turned again, without a word, to leave the room. But as he reached the door Sir James stopped him a second time.

"Stay!" he called. "I had nigh missed telling you somewhat else. My lord has made you a present this morning that ye know not of. It is" —then he stopped for a few moments, perhaps to enjoy the full flavor of what he had to say— "it is a great Flemish horse of true breed and right mettle—a horse such as a knight of the noblest strain might be proud to call his own.

Myles Falworth, ye were born upon a lucky day!"

"Sir," cried Myles, and then stopped short. Then, "Sir," he cried again, "did ye say it—the horse—was to be mine?"

"Aye, it is to be yours."

"My very own?"

"Your very own."

How Myles Falworth left that place he never knew. He was like one in some strange, wonderful dream. He walked upon air, and his heart was so full of joy and wonder and amazement that it thrilled almost to agony. Of course his first thought was of Gascoyne. How he found him he never could tell, but find him he did.

"Come, Francis!" he cried. "I have something to tell you so marvelous that had it come on me from paradise it could not be more strange."

Then he dragged him away to their Eyry—it had been many a long day since they had been there—and to all his friend's speeches, to all his wondering questions, he answered never a word until they had climbed the stairs and came to their old haunt. Then he spoke.

"Sit ye down, Francis," said he, "till I tell you that which passes wonder." As Gascoyne obeyed, he himself stood looking about him. "This is the last time I shall ever come hither," said he. And thereupon he poured out his heart to his listening friend in the murmuring solitude of the airy height. He did not speak of the Earl, but of the wonderful new life that had thus suddenly opened before him, with its golden future of limitless hopes, of dazzling possibilities, of heroic ambitions. He told everything, walking up and down the while—for he could not remain quiet—his cheeks glowing and his eyes sparkling.

Gascoyne sat quite still, staring straight before him. He knew that his friend was ruffling eagle pinions for a flight in which he could never hope to follow, and somehow his heart ached, for he knew that this must be the beginning of the end of the dear, delightful friendship of the year past.

CHAPTER · 22

AND SO ENDED Myles Falworth's boyhood. Three years followed, during which he passed through that state which immediately follows boyhood in all men's lives—a time when they are neither lads nor grown men, but youths passing from the one to the other period through what is often an uncouth and uncomfortable age.

He had fancied, when he talked with Gascoyne in the Eyry, that he was to become a man all at once. He felt just then that he had forever done with boyish things. But that is not the way it happens in men's lives. Changes do not come so suddenly and swiftly as that, but by little and little. For three or four days, maybe, he went his new way of life filled with the great change that had come upon him, and then, now in this and now in that, he drifted back very much into his old ways of boyish doings. As was said, one's young days do not end all at once, even when they are so suddenly and sharply shaken, and Myles was no different from others. He had been stirred to the core by that first wonderful sight of the great and glorious life of manhood opening before him, but he had yet many a sport to enjoy, many a game to play, many a boisterous romp to riot in the dormitory, many an expedition to make to copse and spinney and river on days when he was off duty and when permission had been granted.

Nevertheless, there was a great and vital change in his life—a change which he hardly felt or realized. Even in resuming his old life there was no longer the same vitality, the same zest, the same enjoyment in all these things. It seemed as though they were no longer a part of himself. The savor had gone from them, and by and by it was pleasanter to sit looking on at the sports and the games of the younger lads than to take active part in them.

The three years of his life that had thus passed had been very full—full mostly of work, grinding and monotonous; of training dull, dry, laborious. For Sir James Lee was a taskmaster as hard as iron and seemingly as cold as a stone. For two, perhaps for three, weeks Myles entered into his new exercises with all the enthusiasm that novelty brings. But these exercises hardly varied a little from day to day, and soon became a duty, and finally a hard and grinding task. In the earlier days of his castle life he used to hate the dull monotony of the triweekly hacking at the pels with a heavy broadsword as he hated nothing else. But now, though he still had that exercise to perform, it was almost a relief from the heavy dullness of riding, riding, riding in the tiltyard with shield and lance—couch—recover—*en passant*.

But though now he had but little time for boyish plays and escapades, his life was not altogether without relaxation. Now and then he was permitted to drive in mock battle with other of the younger knights and bachelors in the paddock near the outer walls. It was a still more welcome change in the routine of his life when, occasionally, he would break a light lance in the tilting court with Sir Everard Willoughby while Lord George, perhaps, and maybe one or two others of the Hall folk looked on.

Then one gilded day, when Lord Dudleigh was visiting at Devlen, Myles ran a course with a heavier lance in the presence of the Earl, who came down to the tiltyard with his guest to see the young novitiate ride against Sir Everard. He did his best, and did it well. Lord Dudleigh praised his poise and carriage, and Lord George, who was present, gave him an approving smile and nod. But the Earl of Mackworth only sat stroking his beard impassively, as was his custom. Myles would have given much to know his thoughts.

In all these years Sir James Lee almost never gave any expression either of approbation or disapproval—except when Myles exhibited some carelessness or oversight. Then his words were sharp and harsh enough. More than once Myles' heart failed him, and bitter discouragement took possession of him. Then nothing but his bulldog tenacity and stubbornness brought him out from the despondency of the dark hours.

"Sir," he burst out one day, when his heart was heavy with some failure, "tell me, I beseech you, do I show any skill at all? Is it in me ever to make a worthy knight, fit to hold lance and sword with other men, or am I only a dull, heavy block, worth naught of any good?"

"Ye are a fool, sirrah!" answered Sir James, in his grimmest tones. "Think ye to learn all of knightly prowess in a year and a half? Wait until ye are ripe, and then I will tell you if ye are fit to couch a lance or ride a course with a right knight."

"Ye are an old bear!" muttered Myles to himself, as the one-eyed knight turned on his heel and strode away. "Beshrew me if I show you not that I am as worthy to couch a lance as ye one of these fine days!"

However, during the last of the three years the grinding routine of his training had not been quite so severe as at first. His exercises took him more often out into the fields, and it was during this time of his knightly education that he sometimes rode against some of the castle knights in friendly battle with sword or lance or wooden mace. In these encounters he always held his own; and held it more than well, though, in his boyish simplicity, he was altogether unconscious of his own skill, address, and strength. Perhaps it was his very honest modesty that made him so popular and so heartily liked by all.

He had by this time risen to the place of head squire or chief bachelor, holding the same position that Walter Blunt had occupied when he himself had first come, a raw country boy, to

Devlen. The lesser squires and pages fairly worshiped him as a hero, although they imposed upon his good nature. All took a pride in his practice in knightly exercises, and fabulous tales were current among the young fry concerning his strength and skill.

Yet, although Myles was now at the head of his class, he did not, as other chief bachelors had done, take a leading position among the squires in the Earl's household service. Lord Mackworth, for his own good reasons, relegated him to the position of Lord George's especial attendant. Nevertheless, the Earl always distinguished him from the other esquires, giving him a cool nod whenever they met. Myles, upon his part—now that he had learned better to appreciate how much his lord had done for him—would have shed the last drop of blood in his veins for the head of the house of Beaumont.

As for the two young ladies, he often saw them, and sometimes, even in the presence of the Earl, exchanged a few words with them, and Lord Mackworth neither forbade it nor seemed to notice it.

Toward the Lady Anne he felt the steady, friendly regard of a lad for a girl older than himself. Toward the Lady Alice, now budding into ripe young womanhood, there lay deep in his heart the resolve someday to be her true knight in earnest as he had been her knight in pretense in that time of boyhood when he had so perilously climbed into the privy garden.

In body and form he was now a man, and in thought and heart was quickly ripening to manhood, for, as was said before, men matured quickly in those days. He was a right comely youth, for the promise of his boyish body had been fulfilled in a tall, powerful, well-knit frame. His face was still round and boyish, but on cheek and chin and lip was the curl of adolescent beard—soft, yellow, and silky. His eyes were as blue as steel, and quick and sharp in glance as those of a hawk. As he walked, his arms swung from his broad, square shoulders, and his body swayed with pent-up strength ready for action at any moment.

If little Lady Alice, hearing much talk of his doings and of his promise in these latter times, thought of him now and then, it is not to be wondered at.

Such were the changes that three years had wrought. And from now the story of his manhood really begins.

Perhaps in all the history of Devlen Castle, even at this, the high tide of pride and greatness of the house of Beaumont, the most notable time was in the early autumn of the year 1411, when for five days King Henry IV was entertained by the Earl of Mackworth. The King was at that time making a tour through certain of the midland counties, and with him traveled the Comte de Vermoise. The Count was the secret emissary of the Dauphin's faction in France, at that time in the very bitterest intensity of the struggle with the Duke of Burgundy, and had come to England seeking aid for his master.

It was not the first time that royalty had visited Devlen. Once, in Earl Robert's day, King Edward II had spent a week at the castle during the period of the Scottish wars. But at that time it was little more than a military post, and was used by the King as such. Now the Beaumonts were in the very flower of their prosperity, and preparations were made for the coming visit of royalty upon a scale of such magnificence and splendor as Earl Robert, or perhaps even King Edward himself, had never dreamed.

For weeks the whole castle had been alive with folk hurrying hither and thither, and with the daily and almost hourly coming of packhorses, laden with bales and boxes, from London. From morning to night one heard the ceaseless chip-chipping of the masons' hammers, and saw carriers of stones and mortar ascending and descending the ladders of the scaffolding that covered the face of the great North Hall. Within, that part of the building was alive with the scraping of the carpenters' saws, the clattering of lumber, and the rapping and banging of hammers.

The North Hall had been assigned as the lodging place for the King and his court, and St. George's Hall (as the older building adjoining it was called) had been set apart as the lodging of the Comte de Vermoise and the knights and gentlemen attendant upon him.

The great North Hall had been very much altered and changed for the accommodation of the King and his entourage. A beautiful gallery of carved woodwork had been built within and across the south end of the room for the use of the ladies who were to look down upon the ceremonies below. Two additional windows had been cut through the wall and glazed, and passageways had been opened connecting with the royal apartments beyond. In the bedchamber a bed of carved wood and silver had been built into the wall, and had been draped with hangings of pale blue and silver; and a magnificent screen of wrought iron and carved wood had been erected around the couch. Rich and beautiful tapestries brought from Italy and Flanders were hung upon the walls. Cushions of velvets and silks stuffed with down covered benches and chairs. The floor of the hall was spread with mats of rushes stained in various colors, woven into curious patterns; and in the smaller rooms precious carpets of arras were laid on the cold stones.

All of the cadets of the house had been assembled; all of the gentlemen-in-waiting, retainers and clients. The castle seemed full to overflowing. Even the dormitory of the squires was used as a lodging place for many of the lesser gentry.

So at last, in the midst of all this bustle of preparation, came the day of days when the King was to arrive. The day before a courier had come bringing the news that he was lodging at Donaster Abbey overnight, and would make progress the next day to Devlen.

That morning, as Myles was marshaling the pages and squires, and, with the list of names in his hand, was striving to evolve some order out of the confusion, assigning the various individuals their special duties—these to attend in the household, those to ride in the escort—one of the gentlemen of Lord George's household came with an order for him to come immediately to the young nobleman's apartments. Myles hastily turned over his duties to Gascoyne and Wilkes, and then hurried after the messenger. He found Lord George in the antechamber, three gentlemen squires arming him in a magnificent suit of ribbed Milan steel.

He greeted Myles with a nod and a smile as the lad entered. "Sirrah," said he, "I have had a talk with Mackworth this morning concerning you, and have a mind to do you an honor in my poor way. How would ye like to ride today as my special squire of escort?"

Myles flushed to the roots of his hair. "Oh, sir!" he cried, eagerly, "if I be not too ungainly for your purpose, no honor in all the world could be such joy to me as that!"

Lord George laughed. "A little matter pleases you hugely," said he; "but as to being ungainly, who so says that of you belies you, Myles. You are not ungainly, sirrah. But that is not to the point. I have chosen you for my equerry today, so make ye haste and don your armor, and then come hither again, and Hollingwood will fit you with a wreathed basinet that I have, and a tunic embroidered with my arms and colors."

When Myles had made his bow and left his patron, he flew across the quadrangle and burst into the armory upon Gascoyne, whom he found still lingering there, chatting with one or two of the older bachelors.

"What think ye, Francis?" he cried, wild with excitement. "An honor has been done me this day I could never have hoped to enjoy. Out of all this household, Lord George has chosen me his equerry for the day to ride to meet the

151

King. Come, hasten to help me to arm! Are ye not glad of this thing for my sake, Francis?"

"Aye, glad am I indeed!" cried Gascoyne, that generous friend. "Rather almost would I have this befall you than myself!" And indeed he was hardly less jubilant than Myles over the honor.

Five minutes later he was busy arming him in the little room at the end of the dormitory which had been lately set apart for the use of the head bachelor. "And to think," he said, looking up as he kneeled, strapping the thigh plates to his friend's legs, "that he should have chosen you before all others of the fine knights and lords and gentlemen of quality that are here!"

"Yea," said Myles, "it passes wonder. I know not why he should so single me out for such an honor. It is strangely marvelous."

"Nay," said Gascoyne, "there is no marvel in it, and I know right well why he chooses you. It is because he sees, as we all see, that ye are the stoutest and the best skilled in arms, and most easy of carriage of any man in all this place."

Myles laughed. "If ye make sport of me," said he, "I'll rap your head with this dagger hilt. Ye are a silly fellow, Francis, to talk so. But tell me, have ye heard who rides with my lord?"

"Yea; I heard Wilkes say it was Sir James Lee."

"I am right glad of that," said Myles, "for then he will show me what to do and how to bear myself. It frightens me to think what would happen should I make some mistake in my awkwardness. I think Lord George would never have

152

me with him any more if I do anything amiss this day."

"Never fear," said Gascoyne; "ye will not do anything amiss."

And now, at last, the Earl, Lord George, and all their escort were ready. Then the orders were given to horse, the bugle sounded, and away they all rode, with clashing of hoofs and ringing and jingling of armor, out into the dewy freshness of the early morning, the slant yellow sun of autumn blazing and flaming upon polished helmets and shields, and twinkling like sparks of fire upon spear points. Myles' heart thrilled within him for pure joy, and he swelled out his sturdy young breast with great draughts of the sweet fresh air that came singing across the sunny hilltops. Sir James Lee, who acted as the Earl's equerry for the day, rode at a little distance, and there was an almost pathetic contrast between the grim, steadfast impassiveness of the tough old warrior and Myles' passionate exuberance of youth.

At the head of the party rode the Earl and his brother side by side, each clad cap-a-pie in a suit of Milan armor, the cuirass of each covered with a velvet tunic embroidered in silver with the arms and quarterings of the Beaumonts. The Earl wore around his neck an "S S" collar, with a jeweled St. George hanging from it, and upon his head a vizored basinet, ornamented with a wreath covered with black and yellow velvet and glistening with jewels.

Lord George, as was said before, was clad in a beautiful suit of ribbed Milan armor. It was rimmed with a thin thread of gold, and, like his brother, he wore a basinet wreathed with black and yellow velvet.

Behind the two brothers and their equerries rode the rest in their proper order—knights, gentlemen, esquires, men-at-arms—to the number, perhaps, of two hundred and fifty, spears and lances aslant, and banners, pennons, and flags of black and yellow fluttering in the warm September air.

From the castle to the town they rode, and then across the bridge, and thence clattering up through the stony streets, where people looked down upon them from the windows above, or crowded the fronts of the shops of the tradesmen. Lusty cheers were shouted for the Earl, but the great lord rode staring ever straight before him, as unmoved as a stone. Then out of the town they clattered, and away in a sweeping cloud of dust across the countryside.

It was not until they had reached the windy top of Willoughby Croft, ten miles away, that they met the King and his company. As the two parties approached to within forty or fifty yards of one another, they stopped.

As they came to a halt, Myles observed that a gentleman dressed in a plain blue-gray riding habit, and sitting upon a beautiful white gelding, stood a little in advance of the rest of the party, and he knew that that must be the King. Then Sir James nodded to Myles, and leaping from his horse, flung the reins to one of the attendants. Myles did the same; and then, still following Sir James' lead as he served Lord Mackworth, went forward and held Lord George's stirrup while he dismounted. The two noblemen quickly re-

moved each his basinet, and Myles, holding the
bridle rein of Lord George's horse with his left
hand, took the helmet in his right, resting it upon
his hip.

Then the two brothers walked forward bare-
headed, the Earl a little in advance. Reaching
the King, he stopped, and then bent his knee—
stiffly in the armored plates—until it touched the
ground. Thereupon the King reached him his
hand, and the Earl, rising again, took it, and set
it to his lips.

Then Lord George, advancing, kneeled as his
brother had kneeled, and to him also the King
gave his hand.

Myles could hear nothing, but he could see
that a few words of greeting passed between the
three, and then the King, turning, beckoned to a
knight who stood just behind him and a little
in advance of the others of the troop. In answer, the knight rode forward. The King spoke
a few words of introduction, and the stranger,
ceremoniously drawing off his right gauntlet,
clasped the hand, first of the Earl, and then of
Lord George. Myles knew that he must be the
great Comte de Vermoise, of whom he had
heard so much of late.

A few moments of conversation followed, and
then the King bowed slightly. The French nobleman instantly reined back his horse, an order
was given, and then the whole company moved
forward, the two brothers walking upon either
side of the King, the Earl lightly touching the
bridle rein with his bare hand.

While all this was passing, the Earl of Mackworth's company has been drawn up in a double

line along the roadside, leaving the way open to the other party. As the King reached the head of the troop, another halt followed while he spoke a few courteous words of greeting to some of the lesser nobles attendant upon the Earl whom he knew.

In that little time he was within a few paces of Myles, who stood motionless as a statue, holding the basinet and the bridle rein of Lord George's horse.

What Myles saw was a plain, rather stout man, with a face fat, smooth, and waxy, with pale-blue eyes, and baggy in the lids; clean-shaven, except for a mustache and tuft covering lips and chin. Somehow he felt a deep disappointment. He had expected to see something lionlike, something regal, but instead the great King Henry was commonplace, fat, unwholesome-looking. It came to him with a sort of shock that, after all, a King was in nowise different from other men.

Meanwhile the Earl and his brother replaced their basinets, and presently the whole party moved forward on the way to Devlen.

CHAPTER · 23

THAT SAME AFTERNOON the squires' quarters were thrown into such a ferment of excitement as had, perhaps, never before stirred them. About one o'clock in the afternoon the Earl himself and Lord George came walking slowly across the

Armory Court, wrapped in deep conversation, and entered Sir James Lee's office.

All the usual hubbub of noise that surrounded the neighborhood of the dormitory and the armory was stilled at their coming, and when the two noblemen had entered Sir James' office, the lads and young men gathered in knots discussing with an almost awesome interest what that visit might portend.

After some time Sir James Lee came to the door at the head of the long flight of stone steps, and whistling, beckoned one of the smaller pages to him. He gave a short order that sent the little fellow flying on some mission. In the course of a few minutes he returned, hurrying across the stony court with Myles Falworth, who presently entered Sir James' office. It was then and at this sight that the intense, half-suppressed excitement reached its height of fever heat. What did it all mean? The air was filled with a thousand vague, wild rumors, but the very wildest surmises fell short of the real truth.

Perhaps Myles was somewhat pale when he entered the office. Certainly his nerves were in a tremor, for his heart told him that something very portentous was about to befall him. The Earl sat at the table, and in the seat that Sir James Lee usually occupied, Lord George half sat, half leaned in the window place. Sir James stood with his back to the empty fireplace, his hands clasped behind him. All three were very serious.

"Good day, Myles Falworth," said the Earl, as Myles bowed first to him and then to the others. "I would have you prepare yourself for a great happening." Then, continuing directly to the point: "Ye know, sirrah, why we have been training you so closely these three years gone. It is that ye should be able to hold your own in the world. Nay, not only hold your own, but to show yourself to be a knight of prowess should it come to battle between you and your father's enemy, for there lies no halfway place for you, and ye must be either great or else nothing. Well, sir, the time has now come for you to show your mettle. I would rather have chosen that ye had labored a twelvemonth longer, but now, as I said, has come a chance to prove yourself that may never come again. Sir James tells me that ye are passably ripe in skill. Ye must now show whether that be so or not. Have ye ever heard of the Sieur de la Montaigne?"

"Yea, my lord. I have heard of him often," answered Myles. "It was he who won the prize at the great tourney at Rochelle last year."

"I see that ye have his fame at your tongue's end," said the Earl; "he is the chevalier of whom I speak, and he is reckoned the best knight of Dauphiny. That one of which ye spoke was the third great tourney in which he was adjudged the victor. I am glad that ye hold his prowess highly. Know ye that he is here with the Comte de Vermoise?"

"Nay," said Myles, flushing, "I did hear news he was in England, but knew not that he was in this place."

"Yea," said Lord Mackworth; "he is here." He paused for a moment, then said suddenly, "Tell

158

me, Myles Falworth, if ye were a knight and of rank fit to run a joust with the Sieur de la Montaigne, would ye dare encounter him in the lists?"

The Earl's question fell upon Myles so suddenly and unexpectedly that for a moment or so he stood staring at the speaker with mouth agape. Meanwhile the Earl sat looking calmly back at him, slowly stroking his beard the while.

It was Sir James Lee's voice that broke the silence. "Ye heard your lord speak," said he, harshly. "Have ye no tongue to answer, sirrah?"

"Be silent, Lee," said Lord Mackworth, quietly. "Let the lad have time to think before he speaks."

The sound of the words aroused Myles. He advanced to the table, and rested his hand upon it. "My lord—my lord," said he, "I know not what to say, I—I am amazed and afraid."

"How! how!" cried Sir James Lee, harshly. "Afraid, say ye? If ye are afraid, ye knave, ye need never look upon my face or speak to me more! I have done with you forever if ye are afraid, even were the champion a Sir Alisander."

"Peace, peace, Lee," said the Earl, holding up his hand. "Ye are too hasty. The lad shall have his will in this matter, and ye and no one else shall constrain him. I think, also, ye do not understand him. Speak from your heart, Myles. Why are ye afraid?"

"Because," said Myles, "I am so young, sir. I am but a raw boy. How should I dare be so hardy as to venture to set lance against such a one as the Sieur de la Montaigne? What would

I be but a laughingstock for all the world who would see me so foolish as to venture against one of such prowess and skill?"

"Nay, Myles," said Lord George, "ye think not well enough of your own skill and prowess. Think ye we would undertake to set you against him, if we did not think that ye could hold your own fairly well?"

"Hold my own?" cried Myles, turning to Lord George. "Sir, ye do not mean—ye cannot mean, that I may hope or dream to hold my own against the Sieur de la Montaigne."

"Aye," said Lord George, "that was what I did mean."

"Come, Myles," said the Earl; "now tell me: Will ye fight the Sieur de la Montaigne?"

"Yea," said Myles, drawing himself to his full height and throwing out his chest. "Yea," and his cheeks and forehead flushed red; "if ye bid me do so, I will fight him."

"There spake my brave lad!" cried Lord George heartily.

"I give you joy, Myles," said the Earl, reaching him his hand, which Myles took and kissed. "And I give you double joy. I have talked with the King concerning you this morning, and he has consented to knight you—yea, to knight you with all honors of the Bath—provided ye will match against the Sieur de la Montaigne for the honor of England and Mackworth. Just now the King sleeps for a little while after his dinner. Have yourself in readiness when he comes forth, and I will have you presented."

Then the Earl turned to Sir James Lee, and

questioned him as to how the bachelors were fitted with clothes. Myles listened, only half hearing the words through the tumbling of his thoughts. He had dreamed that sometime he might be knighted, but that time always seemed very distant. To be knighted now, by the King, with the honors of the Bath, and under the patronage of the Earl of Mackworth; to joust —actually joust—with the Sieur de la Montaigne, one of the most famous chevaliers of France! No wonder he only half heard the words, half heard the Earl's questions concerning his clothes and the discussion which followed, half heard Lord George volunteer to array him in fitting garments from his own wardrobe.

"Ye may go now," said the Earl, at last turning to him. "But be ye at George's apartments by two of the clock to be dressed fittingly for the occasion."

Then Myles went out stupefied, dazed, bewildered. He looked around, but he did not see Gascoyne. He said not a word to any of the others in answer to the eager questions poured upon him by his fellow squires, but walked straight away. He hardly knew where he went, but by and by he found himself in a grassy angle below the end of the south stable—a spot overlooking the outer wall and the river beyond. He looked around. No one was near, and he flung himself at length, burying his face in his arms. How long he lay there he did not know, but suddenly someone touched him upon the shoulder, and he sprang up quickly. It was Gascoyne.

"Myles," said his friend, anxiously, "what is

all this talk I hear concerning you up yonder at the armory?"

"Oh, Francis!" cried Myles, in a husky, choking voice, "I am to be knighted—by the King—by the King himself; and I—I am to fight the Sieur de la Montaigne."

He reached out his hand, and Gascoyne took it. They stood for a while quite silent. When at last the stillness was broken, it was Gascoyne who spoke in a choking voice.

"Ye are going to be great, Myles," said he. "I always knew that it must be so with you, and now the time has come. Yea, ye will be great, and live at court among noble folk and kings. Presently ye will not be with me any more, and will forget me by and by."

"Nay, Francis, never will I forget you!" answered Myles, pressing his friend's hand. "I will always love you better than anyone in the world, except only my father and my mother."

Gascoyne shook his head and looked away, swallowing at the dry lump in his throat. Suddenly he turned to Myles. "Will ye grant me a boon?"

"Yea," answered Myles. "What is it?"

"That ye will choose me for your squire."

"Nay," said Myles. "How can ye think to serve me as squire? Ye will be a knight yourself someday, Francis, and why do ye wish now to be my squire?"

"Because," said Gascoyne, with a short laugh, "I would rather be in your company as a squire than in my own as a knight, even if I might be banneret."

Myles flung his arm around his friend's neck,

and kissed him upon the cheek. "Ye shall have your will," said he. "But whether knight or squire, ye are ever my own true friend."

Then they went slowly back to the castle.

At two o'clock Myles went to Lord George's apartments, and there his friend and patron dressed him out in a costume better fitted for the ceremony of presentation—a fur-trimmed jacket of green brocaded velvet embroidered with golden thread, a black velvet hood cap rolled like a turban and with a jewel in the front, a pair of crimson hose, and a pair of black velvet shoes trimmed and stitched with gold thread. Myles had never worn such splendid clothes before, and he could not but feel that they became him well.

"Sir," said he, as he looked down at himself, "sure it is not lawful for me to wear such clothes as these."

In those days there was a law, known as a sumptuary law, which regulated by statute the clothes that each class of people were privileged to wear. It was, as Myles said, against the law for him to wear such garments as those in which he was clad—either velvet, crimson stuff, fur, or silver or gold embroidery—nevertheless such a solemn ceremony as presentation to the King excused the temporary overstepping of the law, and so Lord George told him. As he laid his hand upon the lad's shoulder and held him off at arm's length, he added, "And I pledge you my word, Myles, that ye are as lusty and handsome a lad as ever my eyes beheld."

"Ye are very kind to me, sir," said Myles, in answer.

Lord George laughed, and then giving him a shake, let go his shoulder.

It was about three o'clock when little Edmond de Montefort, Lord Mackworth's favorite page, came with word that the King was then walking in the Earl's pleasance.

"Come, Myles," said Lord George. Myles arose from the seat where he had been sitting, his heart palpitating and throbbing tumultuously.

At the wicket gate of the pleasance two gentlemen-at-arms stood guard in half-armor. They saluted Lord George, and permitted him to pass with his protégé. As he laid his hand upon the latch of the wicket, he paused for a moment and turned.

"Myles," said he, in a low voice, "ye are a thoughtful and cautious lad; for your father's sake be thoughtful and cautious now. Do not speak his name or betray that ye are his son." Then he opened the wicket gate and entered.

Any lad of Myles' age, even one far more used to the world than he, would perhaps have felt all the oppression that he experienced under the weight of such a presentation. He hardly knew what he was doing as Lord George led him to where the King stood, a little apart from the attendants, with the Earl and the Comte de Vermoise. Even in his confusion he knew enough to kneel, and somehow his honest, modest diffidence became him very well. He was not awkward; for one so healthful in mind and body as he could not bear himself very ill, and he felt the assurance that in Lord George he had a kind friend at his side, and one well used to court ceremonies to lend him countenance. Then there is something always pleasing in frank, modest manliness such as was stamped on Myles' handsome, sturdy face. No doubt the King's heart warmed toward the fledgling warrior kneeling in the pathway before him. He smiled very kindly as he gave the lad his hand to kiss, and that ceremony done, held fast to the hard, brown, sinewy fist of the young man with his soft white hand, and raised him to his feet.

"By the Mass!" said he, looking Myles over with smiling eyes, "ye are a right champion in good sooth. Such as ye are was Sir Galahad when he came to Arthur's court. And so they tell me, ye have stomach to brook the Sieur de la Montaigne, that tough old boar of Dauphiny. Have ye the courage to face him? Know ye what a great thing it is that ye have set upon yourself—to do battle, even in sport, with him?"

"Yea, your Majesty," answered Myles, "well I know it is a task perhaps beyond me. But gladly would I take upon me even a greater venture, and one more dangerous, to do your Majesty's pleasure!"

The King looked pleased. "Now that was right well said, young man," said he, "and I like it better that it came from such young and honest lips. Do ye speak French?"

"Yea, your Majesty," answered Myles. "In some small measure I do."

"I am glad of that," said the King; "for so I may make thee acquainted with Sieur de la Montaigne."

He turned as he ended speaking, and beckoned to a heavy, thickset, black-browed chevalier who stood with the other gentlemen attendants at a little distance. He came instantly forward in answer to the summons, and the King introduced the two. As each took the other formally by the hand, he measured his opponent hastily, body and limb, and perhaps each thought that he had never seen a stronger, stouter, better-knit man than the one upon whom he looked. But nevertheless the contrast between the two was very great—Myles, young, boyish, fresh-faced, the other bronzed, weatherbeaten, his face seamed with a great white scar that ran across his forehead and cheek; the one a novice, the other a warrior seasoned in two-score battles.

A few polite phrases passed between the two. The King listened smiling, but with an absent and faraway look gradually stealing over his face. As they ended speaking, a little silence followed, and then the King suddenly aroused himself.

"So," said he, "I am glad that ye two are acquainted. And now we will leave our youthful champion in your charge, Beaumont—and in yours, Mon Sieur, as well—and as soon as the proper ceremonies are ended, we will dub him knight with our own hands. And now, Mackworth, and ye, my lord Count, let us walk a little. I have given further thought to these threescore extra men for Dauphiny."

Then Myles withdrew, under the charge of Lord George and the Sieur de la Montaigne, and while the King and the two nobles walked slowly up and down the gravel path between the tall rosebushes, Myles stood talking with the gentlemen attendants, finding himself, with a certain triumphant exultation, the peer of any and the hero of the hour.

That night was the last that Myles and Gascoyne spent lodging in the dormitory in their squirehood service. The next day they were assigned apartments in Lord George's part of the house, and thither they transported themselves and their belongings, amid the awestruck wonder and admiration of their fellow squires.

CHAPTER · 24

IN MYLES FALWORTH'S DAY one of the greatest ceremonies of courtly life was that of the bestowal of knighthood by the King, with the honors of the Bath. By far the greater number of knights were at that time created by other knights, or by nobles, or by officers of the crown. To be knighted by the King in person distinguished the recipient for life. It was this signal honor that the Earl, for his own purposes, wished Myles to enjoy, and for this end he had laid not a few plans.

The "accolade" was the term used for the creation of a knight upon the field of battle. It was a reward of valor or of meritorious service, and was generally bestowed in a more or less offhand manner. But the ceremony of the Bath was an occasion of the greatest courtly moment, and it was thus that Myles Falworth was to be knighted in addition to the honor of a royal belting.

A quaint old book treating of knighthood and chivalry gives a full and detailed account of all the circumstances of the ceremony of a creation of a Knight of the Bath. It tells us that the candidate was first placed under the care of two squires of honor, "grave and well seen in courtship and nurture, and also in feats of chivalry," which same were likewise to be governors in all things relating to the coming honors.

First of all, the barber shaved Myles, and cut his hair in a certain peculiar fashion ordained for the occasion, the squires of honor supervising the operation. This being concluded, the candidate was solemnly conducted to the chamber where a bath of tepid water was prepared, "hung within and without with linen, and likewise covered with rich cloths and embroidered linen." While in the bath two "ancient, grave, and reverend knights" attended the bachelor, giving him "meet instructions in the order and feats of chivalry." The candidate was then examined as to his knowledge and acquirements, and then, all questions being answered to the satisfaction of his examiners, the elder of the two dipped a handful of water out from the bath, and poured it upon his head, at the same time signing his left shoulder with the sign of the cross.

As soon as this ceremony was concluded, the two squires of honor helped their charge from the bath and conducted him to a plain bed without hangings, where they let him rest until his body was warm and dry. Then they clothed him in a white linen shirt, and over it a plain robe of russet, "girdled about the loins with a rope, and having a hood like unto a hermit's."

As soon as the candidate had arisen, the two "ancient knights" returned, and all being in readiness he was escorted to the chapel, the two walking, one upon either side of him, his squires of honor marching before, and the whole party preceded by "sundry minstrels making a loud noise of music."

When they came to the chapel, the two knights who escorted him took leave of the candidate, each saluting him with a kiss upon the cheek. No one remained with him but his squires of honor, the priest, and the chandler.

In the meantime the novitiate's armor, sword, lance, and helmet had been laid in readiness before the altar. These he watched and guarded while the others slept, keeping vigil until sunrise, during which time "he shall," says the ancient authority, "pass the night in orisons, prayers, and meditation." At daylight he confessed to the priest, heard matins, and communicated in Mass, and then presented a lighted candle at the altar, with a piece of money stuck in it as close to the flame as could be done, the candle being offered to the honor of God, and the money to the honor of that person who was to make him a knight.

So concluded the sacred ceremony, which, being ended, his squires conducted the candidate to his chamber, and there made him comfortable, and left him to repose for a while before the second and final part of the ordinance.

Such is a shortened account of the preparatory stages of the ceremonies through which Myles Falworth passed.

Matters had come upon him so suddenly one after the other, and had come with such bewildering rapidity, that all that week was to him like some strange, wonderful, mysterious vision. He went through it all like one in a dream. Lord George Beaumont was one of his squires of honor; the other, by way of a fitting complement to the courage of the chivalrous lad, was the Sieur de la Montaigne, his opponent soon to be. They were well versed in everything relating to knightcraft, and Myles followed all their directions with passive obedience. Then Sir James Lee and the Comte de Vermoise administered the ceremony of the Bath, the old knight examining him in the laws of chivalry.

It occurs perhaps once or twice in one's lifetime that one passes through great happenings —sometimes of joy, sometimes of dreadful bitterness—in just such a dazed state as Myles passed through this. It is only afterward that all comes back to one so sharply and keenly that the heart thrills almost in agony in living it over again. But perhaps of all the memory of that time, when it afterward came back piece by piece, none was so clear to Myles' back-turned vision as the long night spent in the chapel, watching his armor, thinking such wonderful thoughts, and dreaming such wonderful wide-eyed dreams. At such times Myles saw again the dark mystery of the castle chapel; he saw again the half-moon gleaming white and silvery through the tall, narrow window and throwing a broad form of still whiteness across stone floor, empty seats, and still, motionless figures of stone effigies. At such times he stood again in front of the twinkling tapers that lit the altar where his armor lay piled in a heap, heard again the deep breathing of his companions of the watch sleeping in some empty stall, wrapped each in his cloak, and saw the old chandler bestir himself, and rise and come forward to snuff the candles. At such times he saw again the day growing clearer and clearer through the tall, glazed windows; saw it change to a rosy pink, and then to a broad, ruddy glow that threw a halo of light around Father Thomas' bald head bowed in sleep, and lit up the banners and trophies hanging motionless against the stony face of the west wall; heard again the stirring of life without and the sound of his companions arousing themselves; saw them come forward, and heard them wish him joy that his long watch was ended.

It was nearly noon when Myles was awakened from a fitful sleep by Gascoyne bringing in his dinner, but, as might be supposed, he had but little hunger and ate sparingly. He had hardly ended his frugal meal before his two squires of honor came in, followed by a servant carrying the garments for the coming ceremony. He saluted them gravely, and then, arising, washed his face and hands in a basin which Gascoyne held. Then he kneeled in prayer, the others standing silent at a little distance. As he arose, Lord George came forward.

"The King and the company come presently to the Great Hall, Myles," said he; "it is needful for you to make all the haste that ye are able."

Perhaps never had Devlen Castle seen a more brilliant and goodly company gathered in the Great Hall than that which came to witness King Henry create Myles Falworth a knight bachelor.

At the upper end of the hall was a raised dais, upon which stood a throne covered with crimson satin and embroidered with lions and fleur-de-lis. This was the King's seat. He and his personal attendants had not yet come, but the rest of the company were gathered. The day being warm and sultry, the balcony was all aflutter with the feather fans of the ladies of the family and their attendants, who from this high place looked down upon the hall below. Up the center of the hall was laid a carpet of arras, and the passage was protected by wooden railings. Upon the one side were tiers of seats for the castle gentlefolks and the guests. Upon the other stood the burghers from the town, clad in sober dun and russet, and yeomanry in green and brown. The whole of the great vaulted hall was full of the dull hum of many people waiting, and a ceaseless restlessness stirred the crowded throng. But at last a whisper went around that the King was coming. A momentary hush fell, and through it was heard the noisy clatter of horses' feet coming nearer and nearer, and then stopping before the door. The sudden blare of trumpets broke through the hush, another pause, and then in through the great doorway of the hall came the royal procession.

First of all marched, in the order of their rank, and to the number of a score or more, certain gentlemen, esquires and knights, chosen mostly from the King's attendants. Behind these came two attendants-at-arms in tabards, and following them a part of a dozen or more bannerets and barons. Behind these again, a little space intervening, came two heralds, also in tabards, a group of the greater nobles attendant upon the King following in the order of their rank. Next came the king-at-arms and, at a little distance and walking with sober slowness, the King himself, with the Earl and the Count directly attendant upon him—the one marching on the right hand and the other on the left. A breathless silence filled the whole space as the royal procession advanced slowly up the hall. Through the stillness could be heard the muffled sound of the footsteps on the carpet, the dry rustling of silk and satin garments, and the clear clink and jingle of chains and jeweled ornaments, but not the sound of a single voice.

After the moment or two of bustle and confusion of the King taking his place had passed, another little space of expectant silence fell. At last there suddenly came the noise of acclamation of those who stood without the door—cheering and the clapping of hands—sounds heralding the immediate advent of Myles and his attendants. The next moment the little party entered the hall.

First of all, Gascoyne, bearing Myles' sword in both hands, the hilt resting against his breast, the point elevated at an angle of forty-five degrees. It was sheathed in a crimson scabbard, and the belt of Spanish leather studded with silver bosses was wound around it. From the hilt of the sword dangled the gilt spurs of his coming knighthood. At a little distance behind his squire followed Myles, the center of all observation. He was clad in a novitiate dress, arranged under Lord George's personal supervision. It had been made somewhat different from the fashion usual at such times, and was intended to indicate in a manner the candidate's extreme youthfulness in arms. The outer garment was a tabard robe of white wool, embroidered at the hem with fine lines of silver, and gathered loosely at the waist with a belt of lavender leather stitched with thread of silver. Beneath he was clad in armor (a present from the Earl), new and polished till it shone with dazzling brightness, the breastplate covered with a tunic of white satin, embroidered with silver. Behind Myles, and on either hand came his squires of honor, sponsors, and friends —a little company of some half-dozen in all. As they advanced slowly up the great, dim, high-vaulted room, the whole multitude broke forth into a humming buzz of applause. Then a sudden clapping of hands began near the doorway, ran down through the length of the room, and was taken up by all with noisy clatter.

"Saw I never youth so comely," whispered one of the Lady Anne's attendant gentlewomen. "Sure he looks as Sir Galahad must have looked when he came first to King Arthur's court."

Myles knew that he was very pale. He felt rather than saw the restless crowd of faces on either side, for his eyes were fixed directly before him, upon the dais whereon sat the King, with the Earl of Mackworth standing at his right hand, the Comte de Vermoise at the left, and the others ranged around and behind the throne. It was with the same tense feeling of dreamy unreality that Myles walked slowly up the length of the hall, measuring his steps by those of Gascoyne. Suddenly he felt Lord George Beaumont touch him lightly upon the arm, and almost instinctively he stopped short—he was standing just before the covered steps of the throne.

He saw Gascoyne mount to the third step, stop short, kneel, and offer the sword and the spurs he carried to the King, who took the weapon and laid it across his knees. Then the squire bowed low, and walking backward withdrew to one side, leaving Myles standing alone facing the throne. The King unlocked the spur chains from the sword hilt, and then, holding the gilt spurs in his hand for a moment, he looked Myles straight in the eyes and smiled. Then he turned and gave one of the spurs to the Earl of Mackworth.

The Earl took it with a low bow, turned, and came slowly down the steps to where Myles stood. Kneeling upon one knee, and placing Myles' foot upon the other, Lord Mackworth set the spur in its place and latched the chain over the instep. He drew the sign of the cross upon Myles' bended knee, set the foot back upon the ground, rose with slow dignity, and bowing to the King, withdrew a little to one side.

As soon as the Earl had fulfilled his office the King gave the second spur to the Comte de Vermoise, who set it to Myles' other foot with the same ceremony that the Earl had observed, withdrawing, as he had done, to one side.

A pause of motionless silence followed, and then the King slowly arose and began deliberately to unwind the belt from around the scabbard of the sword he held. As soon as he stood, the Earl and the Count advanced, and taking Myles by either hand, led him forward and up the steps of the dais to the platform above. As they drew a little to one side, the King stooped and buckled the sword belt around Myles' waist; then, rising again, lifted his hand and struck him upon the shoulder, crying in a loud voice,

"Be ye a good knight!"

Instantly a loud sound of applause and the clapping of hands filled the whole hall, in the midst of which the King laid both hands upon Myles' shoulders and kissed him upon the right cheek. So the ceremony ended. Myles was no longer Myles Falworth, but Sir Myles Falworth, Knight by Order of the Bath and by grace of the King!

CHAPTER · 25

IT WAS THE CUSTOM to conclude the ceremonies of the bestowal of knighthood by a grand feast given in honor of the newly created knight. But in Myles' instance the feast was dispensed with. The Earl of Mackworth had planned that Myles might be created a Knight of the Bath with all possible pomp and ceremony; that his personality might be most favorably impressed upon the King; that he might be so honorably knighted as to make him the peer of any who wore spurs in all England; and, finally, that he might celebrate his new honors by jousting with some knight of high fame and approved valor. All these desired plans chance had fulfilled in the visit of the King to Devlen.

As the Earl had said to Myles, he would rather have waited a little while longer until the lad was riper in years and experience, but the opportunity was not to be lost. Young as he was,

Myles must take his chances against the years and grim experience of the Sieur de la Montaigne. But it was also a part of the Earl's purpose that the Knight and Myles should not be brought too intimately together just at that time. Though every particular of circumstance should be fulfilled in the ceremony, it would have been ruination to the Earl's plans to have the knowledge come prematurely to the King that Myles was the son of the attainted Lord Falworth. The Earl knew that Myles was a shrewd, coolheaded lad. But the King had already hinted that the name was familiar to his ears, and a single hasty answer or unguarded speech upon the young knight's part might awaken him to a full knowledge. Such a mishap was, of all things, to be avoided just then; for, thanks to the machinations of that enemy of his father, of whom Myles had heard so much and was soon to hear more, the King had always retained and still held a bitter and rancorous enmity against the unfortunate nobleman.

It was no very difficult matter for the Earl to divert the King's attention from the matter of the feast. His Majesty was very intent just then upon supplying a quota of troops to the Dauphin, and the chief object of his visit to Devlen was to open negotiations with the Earl, looking to that end. He was interested—much interested—in Myles and in the coming jousting in which the young warrior was to prove himself, but he was interested in it by way of a relaxation from the other and more engrossing matter. So, though he made some passing and half-preoccupied inquiry about the feast, he was easily satisfied with the Earl's reasons for not holding it, which were that he had arranged a consultation for that morning in regard to the troops for the Dauphin, to which meeting he had summoned a number of his own more important dependent nobles; that the King himself needed repose and the hour or so of rest that his barber surgeon had ordered him to take after his midday meal; that Father Thomas had laid upon Myles a petty penance—that for the first three days of his knighthood he should eat his meals without meat and in his own apartment; and various other reasons equally good and sufficient. So the King was satisfied, and the feast was dispensed with.

The next morning had been set for the jousting, and all that day the workmen were busy erecting the lists in the great quadrangle upon which, as was said before, looked the main buildings of the castle. The windows of Myles' apartment opened directly upon the bustling scene—the carpenters hammering and sawing; the upholsterers snipping, cutting, and tacking. Myles and Gascoyne stood gazing out from the open casement, with their arms lying across each other's shoulders in the old boyhood fashion, and Myles felt his heart shrink with a sudden tight pang as the realization came sharply and vividly that all these preparations were being made for him, and that the next day he should, with almost the certainty of death, meet either glory or failure under the eyes not only of all the greater and lesser castle folk, but of the King himself and noble strangers critically used to deeds of chivalry and prowess. Perhaps he had never fully realized the magnitude of the reality before. In that tight pang at his heart he drew a deep breath, almost a sigh. Gascoyne turned his head abruptly and looked at his friend, but he did not ask the cause of the sigh. No doubt the same thoughts that were in Myles' mind were in his also.

It was toward the latter part of the afternoon that a message came from the Earl, bidding Myles attend him in his private closet. After Myles had bowed and kissed his lordship's hand, the Earl motioned him to take a seat, telling him that he had some final words to say that might occupy a considerable time. He talked to the young man for about a half-hour in his quiet, measured voice, only now and then showing a little agitation by rising and walking up and down the room for a turn or two. Very many things were disclosed in that talk that caused Myles many long hours of brooding thought, for the Earl spoke freely and without concealment to him concerning his father and the fortunes of the house of Falworth.

Myles had surmised many things, but it was not until then that he knew for a certainty who was his father's malignant and powerful enemy —that it was the great Earl of Alban, the rival and bitter enemy of the Earl of Mackworth. It was not until then that he knew that the present Earl of Alban was the Lord Brookhurst who had killed Sir John Dale in the anteroom at Falworth Castle that morning so long ago in his early childhood. It was not until then that he knew all the circumstances of his father's blindness; that he had been overthrown in the melee at the great tournament at York, and that that same Lord Brookhurst had ridden his iron-shod war horse twice over his enemy's prostrate body before his squire could draw him from the press, and had then and there given him the wound from which he afterward went blind. The Earl swore to Myles that Lord Brookhurst had done what he did willfully, and had afterward boasted of it. Then, with some hesitation, he told Myles the reason for Lord Brookhurst's enmity, and that it had arisen on account of Lady Falworth, whom he had onetime sought in marriage, and that he had sworn vengeance against the man who had won her.

Piece by piece the Earl of Mackworth recounted every circumstance and detail of the revenge that the blind man's enemy had afterward wreaked upon him. He told Myles how, when his father was attainted of high treason, and his estates forfeited to the crown, the King had granted the barony of Easterbridge to the then newly created Earl of Alban in spite of all the efforts of Lord Falworth's friends to the contrary. He told him that when he himself had come out from an audience with the King, with others of his father's friends, the Earl of Alban had boasted in the anteroom, in a loud voice, evidently intended for them all to hear, that now that he had Falworth's fat lands, he would never rest till he had hunted the blind man out from his hiding and brought his head to the block.

"Ever since then," said the Earl of Mackworth, "he has been striving by every means to discover your father's place of concealment. Sometime, perhaps, he may find it, and then—"

Myles had felt for a long time that he was being molded and shaped, and that the Earl of Mackworth's was the hand that was making him what he was growing to be. But he had never realized how great were the things expected of him should he pass the first great test and show himself what his friends hoped to see him. Now he knew that all were looking upon him to act, sometime, as his father's champion, and when that time should come, to challenge the Earl of Alban to the ordeal of single combat, to purge his father's name of treason, to restore him to his rank, and to set the house of Falworth where it stood before misfortune fell upon it.

But it was not alone concerning his and his father's affairs that the Earl of Mackworth talked to Myles. He told him that the Earl of Alban was the Earl of Mackworth's enemy also; that in his younger days he had helped Lord Falworth, who was his kinsman, to win his wife, and that then Lord Brookhurst had sworn to bring about his ruin as he had sworn to ruin Myles' father. He told Myles how, now that Lord Brookhurst was grown to be Earl of Alban, and great and powerful, he was forever plotting against him; and showed Myles how, if Lord Falworth were discovered and arrested for treason, he also would be likely to suffer for aiding and abetting him. Then it dawned upon Myles that the Earl looked to him to champion the house of Beaumont as well as that of Falworth.

"Perhaps," said the Earl, "ye did think that it was all for the pleasant sport of the matter that I have taken upon me this toil and endeavor to have you knighted with honor that ye might fight the Dauphiny knight. Nay, nay, Myles Falworth, I have not labored so hard for such a small matter as that. I have had the King, unknown to himself, so knight you that ye may be the peer of Alban himself, and now I would have you hold your own with the Sieur de la Montaigne, to try whether ye be Alban's match, and to prove yourself worthy of the honor of your knighthood. I am sorry, nevertheless," he added, after a moment's pause, "that this could not have been put off for a while longer, for my plans for bringing you to battle with that vile Alban are not yet ripe. But such a chance of the King's coming hither happens not often. And then I am glad of this much—that a good occasion offers to get you presently away from England. I would have you out of the King's sight as soon as may be after this jousting. He takes a liking to you, and I fear me lest he should inquire more nearly concerning you, and so all be discovered and spoiled. My brother George goes upon the first of next month to France to take service with the Dauphin, having under his command a company of tenscore men— knights and archers. Ye shall go with him, and there stay till I send for you to return."

With this, the protracted interview concluded, the Earl charging Myles to say nothing further about the French expedition for the present— even to his friend—for it was as yet a matter of secrecy, known only to the King and a few nobles closely concerned in the venture.

Then Myles rose to take his leave. He asked and obtained permission for Gascoyne to accompany him to France. Then he paused for a moment or two, for it was strongly upon him to speak of a matter that had been lying in his mind all day—a matter that he had dreamed of much with open eyes during the long vigil of the night before.

The Earl looked up inquiringly. "What is it ye would ask?" said he.

Myles' heart was beating quickly within him at the thought of his own boldness, and as he spoke his cheeks burned like fire. "Sir," said he, mustering his courage at last, "perhaps ye have forgot it, but I have not. Nevertheless, a long time ago when I spoke of serving the—the Lady Alice as her true knight, ye did wisely laugh at my words, and bade me wait first till I had earned my spurs. But now, sir, I have gotten my spurs, and—and do now crave your gracious leave that I may serve that lady as her true knight."

A space of silence fell, in which Myles' heart beat tumultuously within him.

"I know not what ye mean," said the Earl at last, in a somewhat constrained voice. "How would ye serve her? What would ye have?"

"I would have only a little matter just now," answered Myles. "I would but crave of her a favor for to wear in the morrow's battle, so that she may know that I hold her for my own true lady, and that I may have the courage to fight more boldly, having that favor to defend."

The Earl sat looking at him for a while in brooding silence, stroking his beard. Suddenly his brow cleared. "So be it," said he. "I grant you my leave to ask the Lady Alice for a favor, and if she is pleased to give it to you, I shall not say ye nay. But I set this upon you as a provision: that ye shall not see her without the Lady Anne be present. Thus it was, as I remember, ye saw her first, and with it ye must now be satisfied. Go ye to the Long Gallery, and thither they will come if naught hinder them."

Myles waited in the Long Gallery perhaps some fifteen or twenty minutes. No one was there but himself. It was a part of the castle connecting the Earl's and the Countess' apartments, and was used but little. During that time he stood looking absently out of the open casement into the stony courtyard beyond, trying to put into words that which he had to say; wondering, with anxiety, how soon the young ladies would come; wondering whether they would come at all. At last the door at the farther end of the gallery opened, and turning sharply at the sound, he saw the two young ladies enter, the Lady Alice leaning upon the Lady Anne's arm. It was the first time that he had seen them since the ceremony of the morning, and as he advanced to meet them, the Lady Anne came frankly forward and gave him her hand, which Myles raised to his lips.

"I give you joy of your knighthood, Sir Myles," said she, "and do believe, in good sooth, that if anyone deserves such an honor, ye are he."

At first little Lady Alice hung back behind her cousin, saying nothing until the Lady Anne, turning suddenly, said: "Come, cousin, have ye naught to say to our new-made knight? Can ye not also wish him joy of his knighthood?"

The Lady Alice hesitated a minute, then gave Myles a timid hand, which he, with a strange mixture of joy and confusion, took as timidly as it was offered. He raised the hand, and set it lightly and for an instant to his lips, as he had done with the Lady Anne's hand, but with very different emotions.

"I give you joy of your knighthood, sir," said the Lady Alice, in a voice so low that Myles could hardly hear it.

Both flushed red, and as he raised his head again, Myles saw that the Lady Anne had withdrawn to one side. Then he knew that it was to give him the opportunity to proffer his request.

A little space of silence followed, while he strove to key his courage to the saying of that which lay on his mind. "Lady," said he at last, and then again—"Lady, I—have a favor to ask of you."

"What is it ye would have, Sir Myles?" she murmured in reply.

"Lady," said he, "ever since I first saw you I have thought that if I might choose of all the world, ye only would I choose for—for my true lady, to serve as a right knight should." Here he stopped, frightened at his own boldness. The Lady Alice stood quite still, with her face turned away.

"Ye—ye are not angered at what I say?" he said.

She shook her head.

"I have longed and longed for the time," said he, "to ask a boon of you, and now has that time come. Lady, tomorrow I go to meet a right good knight, and one skilled in arms and in jousting, as ye do know. Yea, he is famous in arms, and I be nobody. Nevertheless, I fight for the honor of England and Mackworth—and—and for your sake. I— Ye are not angered at what I say?"

Again the Lady Alice shook her head.

"I would that ye—I would that ye would give me some favor for to wear—your veil or your necklace."

He waited anxiously for a little while, but Lady Alice did not answer immediately.

"I fear me," said Myles presently, "that I have offended you in asking this thing. I know that it is a bold matter for one so raw in chivalry and in courtliness as I am, and one so poor in rank, to ask you for your favor. If I have offended, I prithee let it be as though I had not asked it."

Perhaps it was the young man's timidity that brought a sudden courage to Lady Alice. Perhaps it was the graciousness of her gentle breeding that urged her to relieve Myles' somewhat awkward humility. Perhaps it was something more than either that lent her bravery to speak, even knowing that the Lady Anne heard all. She turned quickly to him. "Nay, Sir Myles," she said, "I am foolish, and do wrong you by my foolishness and silence, for truly I am proud to have ye wear my favor." As she spoke, she unclasped the thin gold chain from about her neck.

"I give you this chain," said she, "and it will bring me joy to have it honored by your true knightliness, and giving it, I do wish you all success."

Then she bowed her head, and turning, left him holding the necklace in his hand.

The Lady Anne left the window to meet her, bowing her head with a smile to Myles as she took her cousin's arm again and led her away. He stood looking after them as they left the room, and when they were gone, he raised the necklace to his lips with a heart beating tumultuously with a triumphant joy it had never felt before.

CHAPTER · 26

AND NOW AT LAST had come the day of days for Myles Falworth, the day when he was to put to the test all that he had acquired in the three years of his training, the day that was to disclose what promise of future greatness there was in his strong young body. And it was a noble day, one of those of late September when the air seems sweeter and fresher than at other times; the sun bright and as yellow as gold; the wind lusty and strong, before which the great white clouds go sailing majestically across the bright blueness of the sky above, while their dusky shadows skim across the brown face of the rusty earth beneath.

As was said before, the lists had been set up in the great quadrangle of the castle, level and smooth as a floor, a fitting place. The course was of the usual size—sixty paces long—and separated along its entire length by a barrier about five feet high. On the west side of the course, and about twenty paces distant from it, a scaffolding had been built facing toward the east so as to avoid the glare of the afternoon sun. In the center was a raised dais, hung round with cloth of blue embroidered with lions rampant. Upon the dais stood a cushioned throne for the King, and upon the steps below, ranged in the order of their dignity, were seats for the Earl, his guests, the family, the ladies, knights, and gentlemen of the castle. In front, the scaffolding was covered with the gayest tapestries and brightest-colored hangings that the castle could afford. And above, particolored pennants and streamers, surmounted by the royal ensign of England, waved and fluttered in the wind.

At either end of the lists stood the pavilions of the knights. That of Myles was at the southern extremity, and was hung, by the Earl's desire, with cloth of the Beaumont colors (black and yellow), while a wooden shield bearing three goshawks spread (the crest of the house) was nailed to the roof, and a long streamer of black and yellow trailed out in the wind from the staff above. Myles, partly armed, stood at the doorway of the pavilion, watching the folk gathering at the scaffolding. The ladies of the house were already seated, and the ushers were bustling hither and thither, assigning the others their places. A considerable crowd of common folk and burghers from the town had already gathered at the barriers opposite, and as he looked at the restless and growing multitude he felt his heart beat quickly and his flesh grow cold with a nervous trepidation.

Suddenly there came a loud blast of trumpets. A great gate at the farther extremity of the lists was thrown open, and the King appeared, riding on a white horse, preceded by the king-at-arms and the heralds, attended by the Earl and the Comte de Vermoise, and followed by a crowd of attendants. Just then Gascoyne, who, with Wilkes, was busy lacing some of the armor plates with new thongs, called Myles, and he turned and entered the pavilion.

As the two squires were adjusting these last pieces, strapping them in place and tying the thongs, Lord George and Sir James Lee entered the pavilion. Lord George took the young man by the hand, and with a pleasant smile wished him success in the coming encounter.

Sir James seemed anxious and disturbed. He said nothing, and after Gascoyne had placed the open basinet that supports the tilting helm in its place, he came forward and examined the armor piece by piece, carefully and critically, testing the various straps and leather points and thongs to make sure of their strength.

"Sir," said Gascoyne, who stood by watching him anxiously, "I do trust that I have done all meetly and well."

"I see nothing amiss, sirrah," said the old knight, half grudgingly. "So far as I may know, he is ready to mount."

Just then a messenger entered, saying that the King was seated, and Lord George bade Myles make haste to meet the challenger.

"Francis," said Myles, "prithee give me my pouch yonder."

Gascoyne handed him the velvet bag, and he

opened it and took out the necklace that the Lady Alice had given him the day before.

"Tie this around my arm," said he. He looked down, keeping his eyes studiously fixed on Gascoyne's fingers as they twined the thin golden chain around the iron plates of his right arm, knowing that Lord George's eyes were upon him, and blushing fiery red at the knowledge.

Sir James was at that moment examining the great tilting helm, and Lord George watched him, smiling amusedly. "And have ye then already chosen yourself a lady?" he said, presently.

"Aye, my lord," answered Myles, simply.

"Marry, I trust we be so honored that she is one of our castle folk," said the Earl's brother.

For a moment Myles did not reply. Then he looked up.

"My lord," said he, "the favor was given to me by the Lady Alice."

Lord George looked grave for the moment. Then he laughed.

"Marry, ye are a bold archer to shoot for such high game."

Myles did not answer, and at that moment two grooms led his horse up to the door of the pavilion. Gascoyne and Wilkes helped him to his saddle, and then, Gascoyne holding his horse by the bridle rein, he rode slowly across the lists to the little open space in front of the scaffolding and the King's seat, just as the Sieur de la Montaigne approached from the opposite direction.

As soon as the two knights champion had reached each his appointed station in front of the scaffolding, the marshal bade the speaker read the challenge. Unrolling the parchment, he began to do so in a loud, clear voice, so that all might hear. It was a quaint document, wrapped up in the tangled heraldic verbiage of the time. The pith of the matter was that the Sieur Brian Philip Francis de la Montaigne proclaimed before all men the greater chivalry and skill at arms of the knights of France and of Dauphiny, and likewise the greater fairness of the ladies of France and Dauphiny, and would there defend those sayings with his body without fear or attaint as to the truth of the same. As soon as the speaker had ended, the marshal bade him call the defendant of the other side.

Then Myles spoke his part, with a voice trembling somewhat with the excitement of the moment, but loudly and clearly enough: "I, Myles Edward Falworth, knight, so created by the hand and by the grace of his Majesty King Henry IV of England, do take upon me the gage of this battle, and will defend with my body the chivalry of the knights of England and the fairness of the ladies thereof!"

Then, after the speaker had ended his proclamation and had retired to his place, the ceremony of claiming and redeeming the helmet, to which all young knights were subjected upon first entering the lists, was performed.

One of the heralds cried in a loud voice, "I, Gilles Hamerton, herald to the most noble Clarencieux, king-at-arms, do claim the helm of Sir Myles Edward Falworth by this reason, that he has never yet entered joust or tourney."

To which Myles answered, "I do acknowl-edge the right of that claim, and herewith proffer in ransom for the same this purse of one hundred marks in gold."

As he spoke, Gascoyne stepped forward and delivered the purse to the herald. It was a more than usually considerable ransom, and had been made up by the Earl and Lord George that morning.

"Right nobly have ye redeemed your helm," said the herald, "and hereafter be ye free to enter any jousting whatsoever, and in whatever place."

So, all being ended, both knights bowed to the King, and then, escorted each by his squire, returned to his pavilion, saluted by the spectators with a loud clapping of hands.

Sir James Lee met Myles in front of his tent. Coming up to the side of the horse, the old man laid his hand upon the saddle, looking up into the young man's face.

"Ye will not fail in this venture and bring shame upon me?" said he.

"Nay, my dear master," said Myles; "I will do my best."

"I doubt it not," said the old man; "and I believe ye will come off right well. From what he did say this morning, I think the Sieur de la Montaigne means only to break three lances with you, and will content himself therewith, without seeking to unhorse you. Nevertheless, be ye bold and watchful, and if ye find that he endeavor to cast you, do your best to unhorse him. Remember also those things which I have told you ten thousand times before: hold your toes well down and grip the stirrup hard, more especially at the moment of meeting; bend your body forward, and keep your elbow close to your side; bear your lance point one foot above your adversary's helm until within two lengths of meeting, and strike ye in the very middle of his shield. So, Myles, ye may hold your own, and come off with glory."

As he ended speaking he drew back, and Gascoyne, mounting upon a stool, covered his friend's head and basinet with the great jousting helm, making fast the leather points that held it to the iron collar.

As he was tying the last thong a messenger came from the herald, saying that the challenger was ready. Then Myles knew the time had come. Reaching down and giving Sir James a grip of the hand, he drew on his gauntlet, took the jousting lance that Wilkes handed him, and turned his horse's head toward his end of the lists.

CHAPTER · 27

As MYLES TOOK HIS PLACE at the south end of the lists, he found the Sieur de la Montaigne already at his station. Through the peephole in the face of the huge helmet, a transverse slit known as the ocularium, he could see, like a strange narrow picture, the farther end of the lists, the spectators upon either side moving and shifting with ceaseless restlessness, and in the center of all, his opponent, sitting with spear point directed upward, erect, motionless as a statue of iron, the sunlight gleaming and flashing upon his polished plates of steel, and the trappings of his horse swaying and fluttering in the rushing of the fresh breeze.

Upon that motionless figure his sight gradually centered with every faculty of mind and soul. He knew the next moment the signal would be given that was to bring him either glory or shame from that iron statue. He ground his teeth together with stern resolve to do his best in the coming encounter, and murmured a brief prayer in the hollow darkness of his huge helm. Then, with a shake, he settled himself more firmly in his saddle, slowly raised his spear point until the shaft reached the exact angle, and there suffered it to rest motionless. There was a moment of dead, tense, breathless pause; then he rather felt than saw the marshal raise his baton. He gathered himself together, and the next moment a bugle sounded loud and clear. In one blinding rush he drove his spurs into the sides of his horse, and in instant answer felt the noble steed spring forward with a bound.

Through all the clashing of his armor reverberating in the hollow depths of his helmet he saw the mail-clad figure from the other end of the lists rushing toward him, looming larger and larger as they came together. He gripped his saddle with his knees, clutched the stirrups with the soles of his feet, and bent his body still more forward. In the instant of meeting, with almost the blindness of instinct, he dropped the point of his spear against the single red fleur-de-lis in the middle of the oncoming shield. There was a thunderous crash that seemed to rack every joint. He heard the crackle of splintered wood, and felt the momentary trembling recoil of the horse beneath him. In the next instant he had passed by. As he checked the onward rush of his horse at the far end of the course, he heard faintly in the dim, hollow recess of the helm the loud shout and the clapping of hands of those who looked on, and found himself gripping with nervous intensity the butt of a broken spear, his mouth clammy with excitement and his heart thumping in his throat.

Then he realized that he had met his opponent, and had borne the meeting well. As he turned his horse's head toward his own end of the lists, he saw the other trotting slowly back toward his station, also holding a broken spear shaft in his hand.

As he passed the iron figure a voice issued from the helmet, "Well done, Sir Myles, nobly done!" and his heart bounded in answer to the words of praise. When he had reached his own end of the lists, he flung away his broken spear, and Gascoyne came forward with another.

"Oh, Myles!" he said, with a sob in his voice, "it was nobly done. Never did I see a better ridden course in all my life. I did not believe that ye could do half so well. Oh, Myles, prithee knock him out of his saddle if ye love me!"

Myles, in his high-keyed nervousness, could not forbear a short, hysterical laugh at his friend's warmth of enthusiasm. He took the fresh lance in his hand, and then, seeing that his opponent was walking his horse slowly up and down at his end of the lists, did the same during the little time of rest before the next encounter.

When, in answer to the command of the marshal, he took his place a second time, he found himself calmer and more collected than before, but every faculty no less intensely fixed than it had been at first. Once more the marshal raised his baton, once more the horn sounded, and once more the two rushed together with the same thunderous crash, the same splinter of broken spears, the same momentary trembling recoil of the horse, and the same onward rush past each other. Once more the spectators applauded and shouted as the two knights turned their horses and rode back toward their stations.

This time as they met midway the Sieur de la Montaigne reined in his horse. "Sir Myles," said his muffled voice, "I swear to you, by my faith, I had not thought to meet in you such an opponent as ye do prove yourself to be. I had thought to find in you a raw boy, but find instead a Paladin. Hitherto I have given you grace as I would give grace to any mere lad, and thought of nothing but to give you opportunity to break your lance. Now I shall do my best to unhorse you as I would an acknowledged peer in arms. Nevertheless, on account of your youth, I give you this warning, so that ye may hold yourself in readiness."

"I give you gramercy for your courtesy, my lord," answered Myles, speaking in French; "and I will strive to encounter you as best I may, and pardon me if I seem forward in so saying, but were I in your place, my lord, I would change yonder breastpiece and overgirth of my saddle; they are sprung in the stitches."

"Nay," said the Sieur de la Montaigne, laugh-

197

ing; "breastpiece and overgirth have carried me through more tilts than one, and shall through this. If ye give me a blow so true as to burst breastpiece and overgirth, I will own myself fairly conquered by you." So saying, he saluted Myles with the butt of the spear he still held, and passed by to his end of the lists.

Myles, with Gascoyne running beside him, rode across to his pavilion, and called to Edmund Wilkes to bring him a cup of spiced wine. After Gascoyne had taken off his helmet, and as he sat wiping the perspiration from his face, Sir James came up and took him by the hand.

"My dear boy," said he, gripping the hand he held, "never could I hope to be so overjoyed in my old age as I am this day. Ye do bring honor to me, for I tell you truly ye do ride like a knight seasoned in twenty tourneys."

"It gives me tenfold courage to hear ye say so, dear master," answered Myles. "And truly," he added, "I shall need all my courage in this bout, for the Sieur de la Montaigne tells me that he will ride to unhorse me this time."

"Did he indeed say so?" said Sir James. "Then likely he means to strike at your helm. Your best chance is to strike also at his. Does your hand tremble?"

"Not now," answered Myles.

"Then keep your head cool and your eye true. Set your trust in God, and happily ye will come out of this bout honorably in spite of the rawness of your youth."

Just then Edmund Wilkes presented the cup of wine to Myles, who drank it off at a draught, and thereupon Gascoyne replaced the helm and tied the thongs.

The charge that Sir James Lee had given to Myles to strike at his adversary's helm was a piece of advice he probably would not have given to so young a knight, except as a last resort. A blow perfectly delivered upon the helm was of all others the most difficult for the recipient to recover from, but then a blow upon the helm was not one time in fifty perfectly given. The huge cylindrical tilting helm was so constructed in front as to slope at an angle in all directions to one point. That point was the center of a cross formed by two iron bands welded to the steelface plates of the helm where it was weakened by the opening slit of the ocularium, or peephole. In the very center of this cross was a little flattened surface where the bands were riveted together, and it was upon that minute point that the blow must be given to be perfect, and that stroke Myles determined to attempt.

As he took his station Edmund Wilkes came running across from the pavilion with a lance that Sir James had chosen, and Myles, returning the one that Gascoyne had just given him, took it in his hand. It was of seasoned oak, somewhat thicker than the other, a tough weapon, not easily to be broken even in such an encounter as he was likely to have. He balanced the weapon, and found that it fitted perfectly to his grasp. As he raised the point to rest, his opponent took his station at the farther extremity of the lists, and again there was a little space of breathless pause. Myles was surprised at his own coolness. Every nervous tremor was gone. Before, he had been conscious of the critical multitude looking down upon him; now it was a conflict of man to man, and such a conflict had no terrors for his young heart of iron.

The spectators had somehow come to the knowledge that this was to be a more serious encounter than the two which had preceded it, and a breathless silence fell for the moment or two that the knights stood in place.

Once more he breathed a short prayer, "Holy Mary, guard me!"

Then again, for the third time, the marshal raised his baton, and the horn sounded, and for the third time Myles drove his spurs into his horse's flanks. Again he saw the iron figure of his opponent rushing nearer, nearer, nearer. He centered, with a straining intensity, every faculty of soul, mind, and body upon one point— the cross of the ocularium, the mark he was to strike. He braced himself for the tremendous shock which he knew must meet him, and then in a flash dropped the lance point straight and true. The next instant there was a deafening, stunning crash—a crash like the stroke of a thunderbolt. There was a dazzling blaze of blinding light, and a myriad sparks danced and flickered and sparkled before his eyes. He felt his horse stagger under him with the recoil, and hardly knowing what he did, he drove his spurs deep into its sides with a shout. At the same moment there resounded in his ears a crashing rattle and clatter, he knew not of what, and then, as his horse recovered and sprang forward, and as the stunning bewilderment passed, he found that his helmet had been struck off. He heard a great shout arise from all, and thought, with a sickening, bitter disappointment, that it was because he had lost. At the farther end of the course he turned his horse, and then his heart gave a leap and a bound as though it would burst, the blood leaped to his cheeks tingling, and he thrilled with an almost agonizing pang of triumph, of wonder, of amazement.

There, in a tangle of his horse's harness and of embroidered trappings, the Sieur de la Montaigne lay stretched upon the ground, with his saddle nearby. His riderless horse was trotting aimlessly about at the farther end of the lists.

Myles saw the two squires of the fallen knight run across to where their master lay; he saw the ladies waving their kerchiefs and veils, and the castle people swinging their hats and shouting in an ecstasy of delight. Then he rode slowly back to where the squires were now aiding the fallen knight to rise. The senior squire drew his dagger, cut the leather points, and drew off the helm, disclosing the knight's face— a face white as death, and convulsed with rage, mortification, and bitter humiliation.

"I was not rightly unhorsed!" he cried, hoarsely, and with livid lips, to the marshal and his attendants, who had ridden up. "I unhelmed him fairly enough, but my overgirth and breast-strap burst, and my saddle slipped. I was not unhorsed, I say, and I lay claim that I unhelmed him."

"Sir," said the marshal calmly, and speaking in French, "surely ye know that the loss of helmet does not decide an encounter. I need not remind you, my lord, that it was so awarded by John of Gaunt, Duke of Lancaster, when in the jousting match between Reynand de Roye and John de Holland the Sieur Reynand left every point of his helm loosened, so that the helm was beaten off at each stroke. If he then was justified in doing so of his own choice, and willfully suffering to be unhelmed, how then can this knight be accused of evil who suffered it by chance?"

"Nevertheless," said the Sieur de la Montaigne, in the same hoarse, breathless voice, "I do affirm, and will make my affirmation good with my body, that I fell only by the breaking of my girth. Who says otherwise lies!"

"It is the truth he speaks," said Myles. "I myself saw the stitches were some little burst, and warned him thereof before we ran this course."

"Sir," said the marshal to the Sieur de la Montaigne, "how can you now complain of that thing which your own enemy advised you of and warned you against? Was it not right knightly for him so to do?"

The Sieur de la Montaigne stood quite still for a little while, leaning on the shoulder of his chief squire, looking moodily upon the ground. Then, without making answer, he turned and walked slowly away to his pavilion, still leaning on his squire's shoulder, while the other attendant followed behind, bearing his shield and helmet.

Gascoyne had picked up Myles' fallen helmet as the Sieur de la Montaigne moved away, and Lord George and Sir James Lee came walking across the lists to where Myles still sat. Then, the one taking his horse by the bridle rein and the other walking beside the saddle, they led him before the raised dais where the King sat.

Even the Comte de Vermoise, mortified and amazed as he must have been at the overthrow of his best knight, joined in the praise and congratulation that poured upon the young conqueror. Myles, his heart swelling with a passion of triumphant delight, looked up and met the gaze of the Lady Alice fixed intently upon him. A red spot of excitement still burned in either cheek, and it flamed to a rosier red as he bowed his head to her before turning away.

Gascoyne had just removed Myles' breast-plate and gorget when Sir James Lee burst into the pavilion. All his grim coldness was gone, and he flung his arms around the young man's neck, hugging him heartily, and kissing him upon either cheek.

Before he let him go, "My own dear boy," he said, holding him off at arm's length and winking his one keen eye rapidly, as though to wink away a dampness of which he was ashamed— "my own dear boy, I do tell you truly this is as sweet to me as though ye were my own son; sweeter to me than when I first broke my own lance in triumph, and felt myself to be a right knight."

"Sir," answered Myles, "what ye say rejoices my very heart. Nevertheless, it is but just to say that both his breastpiece and overgirth were burst in the stitches before he ran his course, for so I saw with my own eyes."

"Burst in the stitches!" snorted Sir James. "Think ye he did not know in what condition was his horse's gearing? I tell you he went down because ye did strike fair and true, and he did not so strike you. Had he been Guy of Warwick he had gone down all the same under such a stroke and in such a case."

CHAPTER · 28

IT WAS NOT UNTIL more than three weeks after the King had left Devlen Castle that Lord George and his company of knights and archers were ready for the expedition to France. Two weeks of that time Myles spent at Crosbey-Dale with his father and mother. It was the first time that he had seen them since, four years ago, he had quitted the low, narrow, white-walled farmhouse for the castle of the great Earl of Mackworth. He had never realized before how low and narrow and poor the farmhouse was. Now, with his eyes trained at the bigness of Devlen Castle, he looked around him with wonder and pity at his father's humble surroundings. He realized as he never else could have realized how great was the fall in fortune that had cast the house of Falworth down from its rightful station to such a level as that upon which it now rested. And at the same time that he thus recognized how poor was their lot, how dependent upon the charity of others, he also recognized how generous was the friendship of Prior Edward, who endangered his own safety so greatly in affording the family of the attainted lord an asylum in its bitter hour of need and peril.

Myles paid many visits to the gentle old priest during the two weeks' visit, and had many long and serious talks with him. One warm bright afternoon, as he and the old man walked together in the priory garden, after a game or two of drafts, the young knight talked more freely and openly of his plans, his hopes, and his ambitions than perhaps he had ever done. He told the old man all that the Earl had disclosed to him concerning the fallen fortunes of his father's house, and of how all who knew those circumstances looked to him to set the family in its old place once more. Prior Edward added many things to those which Myles already knew—things of which the Earl either did not know or did not choose to speak. He told the young man, among other matters, the reason for the bitter and lasting enmity that the King felt for the blind nobleman; that Lord Falworth had been one of King Richard's council in times past; that it was not a little owing to him that King Henry, when Earl of Derby, had been banished from England, and that, though he was then living in the retirement of private life, he bitterly and steadfastly opposed King Richard's abdication. He told Myles that at the time when Sir John Dale found shelter at Falworth Castle, vengeance was ready to fall upon his father at any moment, and it needed only such a pretext as that of sheltering so prominent a conspirator as Sir John to complete his ruin.

Myles, as he listened intently, could not but

confess in his own mind that the King had many rational, perhaps just, grounds for grievance against such an ardent opponent as the blind lord had shown himself to be.

"But, sir," said he, after a little space of silence, when Prior Edward had ended, "to hold enmity and to breed treason are very different matters. My father was Bolingbroke's enemy, but surely ye do not believe he is justly and rightfully tainted with treason?"

"Nay," answered the priest, "how can ye ask me such a thing? If I believed your father a traitor, think ye I would thus tell his son thereof? Nay, Myles, I know your father well, and have known him for many years, and this of him, that few men are so honorable in heart and soul as he. But I have told you all these things to show that the King is not without some reason to be unfriendly to your father. Neither is the Earl of Alban without cause for enmity against him. So ye, upon your part, should not feel bitter rancor against the King for what has happened to your house, nor even against William Brookhurst—I mean the Earl of Alban—for, I tell you, the worst of our enemies and the worst of men believe themselves always to have right and justice upon their side, even when they most wish evil to others."

So spoke the gentle old priest, who looked from his peaceful haven with dreamy eyes upon the sweat and tussle of the world's battle. Had he instead been in the thick of the fight, it might have been harder for him to believe that his enemies ever had right upon their side.

"But tell me this," said Myles presently, "do

ye then think that I do evil in seeking to do a battle of life or death with this wicked Earl of Alban, who has so ruined my father in body and fortune?"

"Nay," said Prior Edward, thoughtfully, "I say not that ye do evil. War and bloodshed seem hard and cruel matters to me. But God has given that they be in the world, and may He forbid that such a poor worm as I should say that they be all wrong and evil."

Myles did not fully understand what the old man meant, but this much he gathered, that his spiritual father did not think ill of his fighting the Earl of Alban for his temporal father's sake.

So Myles went to France in Lord George's company, a soldier of fortune, as his captain was. He was there for only six months, but those six months wrought a great change in his life. In the fierce factional battles that raged around the walls of Paris, in the evil life which he saw at the Burgundian court in Paris itself after the truce—a court brilliant and wicked, witty and cruel—the wonderful liquor of youth had evaporated rapidly, and his character had crystallized as rapidly into the hardness of manhood. The warfare, the blood, the evil pleasures which he had seen had been a fiery, crucible test to his soul. He was no longer the innocent Sir Galahad who had walked in pure white up the Great Hall to be knighted by the King, but his soul was of that grim, sterling, rugged sort that looked out calmly upon the wickedness and debauchery around him, and loved it not.

Then one day a courier came, bringing a

packet. It was a letter from the Earl, bidding Myles return straightway to England and to Mackworth House upon the Strand, near London, without delay, and Myles knew that his time had come.

It was a bright day in April when he and Gascoyne rode clattering out through Temple Bar, leaving behind them quaint old London town, its blank stone wall, its crooked, dirty streets, its high-gabled wooden houses, over which rose the sharp spire of St. Paul's towering high into the golden air. Before them stretched the straight, broad highway of the Strand—on one side the great houses and palaces of princely priests and powerful nobles; on the other the Covent Garden (or the Convent Garden, as it was then called) and the rolling country, where great stone windmills swung their slow-moving arms in the damp, soft April breeze; and away in the distance the Scottish Palace, the White Hall, and Westminster.

It was the first time that Myles had seen famous London town. He jogged along with Gascoyne, gazing about him with calm interest at open shops and booths and tall, gabled houses; at the busy throng of merchants and craftsmen, jostling and elbowing one another; at townsfolk —men and women—picking their way along the muddy kennel of a sidewalk. He had seen so much of the world that he had lost somewhat of interest in new things. So he did not care to tarry, but rode, with a mind heavy with graver matters, through the streets and out through the Temple Bar direct for Mackworth House, near the Savoy Palace.

It was with a great deal of interest that Myles and his patron regarded each other when they met for the first time after that half-year which the young soldier had spent in France. To Myles it seemed somehow very strange that his lordship's familiar face and figure should look so exactly the same. To Lord Mackworth, perhaps, it seemed even more strange that six short months should have wrought so great a change in the young man. The rugged exposure in camp and field during the hard winter that had passed had roughened the smooth bloom of his boyish complexion and bronzed his fair skin almost as much as a midsummer's sun could have done. His beard and mustache had grown again (now heavier and more mannish from having been shaved), and the white seam of a scar over the right temple gave, if not a stern, at least a determined look to the strong, square-jawed young face. So the two stood for a while regarding each other. Myles was the first to break the silence.

"My lord," said he, "ye did send for me to come back to England. Here I am."

"When did ye land, Sir Myles?" said the Earl.

"I and my squire landed at Dover upon Tuesday last," answered the young man.

The Earl of Mackworth stroked his beard softly. "Ye are marvelous changed," said he. "I would not have thought it possible."

Myles smiled somewhat grimly.

"I have seen such things, my lord, in France and in Paris," said he, quietly, "as may make a lad a man before his time."

"From which I gather," said the Earl, "that

many adventures have befallen you. I thought ye would find troublesome times in the Dauphin's camp, else I would not have sent you to France."

A little space of silence followed, during which the Earl sat musingly, half absently, regarding the tall, erect, powerful young figure standing before him, awaiting his pleasure in motionless, patient, almost dogged silence. The strong, sinewy hands were clasped and rested upon the long, heavy sword, around the scabbard of which the belt was loosely wrapped, and the plates of mail caught and reflected in flashing, broken pieces the bright sunlight from the window behind.

"Sir Myles," said the Earl suddenly, breaking the silence at last, "do ye know why I sent for you?"

"Aye," said Myles, calmly, "how can I else? Ye would not have called me from Paris but for one thing. I think ye have sent for me to fight the Earl of Alban, and lo! I am here."

"Ye speak very boldly," said the Earl. "I do hope that your deeds be as bold as your words."

"That," said Myles, "ye must ask other men. No one may justly call me coward."

"By my troth!" said the Earl, smiling. "Looking upon you—limbs and girth, bone and sinew—I would not like to be the one that would dare accuse you of such a thing. As for your surmise, I may tell you plain that ye are right, and that it was to fight the Earl of Alban I sent for you. The time is now nearly ripe, and I will straightway send for your father to come to London. Meantime, it would not be safe either for you or for me to keep you in my service. I have spoken to his Highness the Prince of Wales, who, with other of the princes, is upon our side in this quarrel. He has promised to take you into his service until the fitting time comes to bring you and your enemy together, and to-morrow I shall take you to Scotland Yard, where his Highness is now lodging."

As the Earl ended his speech, Myles bowed, but did not speak. The Earl waited for a little while, as though to give him the opportunity to answer.

"Well, sirrah," said he at last, with a shade of impatience, "have ye naught to say? Ye take all this with marvelous coolness."

"Have I then my lord's permission to speak my mind?"

"Aye," said the Earl, "say your say."

"Sir," said Myles, "I have thought and pondered this matter much while abroad, and would now ask a plain question in all honesty if I have your leave."

The Earl nodded his head.

"Sir, am I not right in believing that ye have certain weighty aims of your own to gain if I win this battle against the Earl of Alban?"

"Has my brother George been telling you aught to such a purpose?" said the Earl, after a moment or two of silence.

Myles did not answer.

"No matter," added Lord Mackworth. "I will not ask who told you such a thing. As for your question—well, since ye ask it frankly, I will be frank with you. Yea, I have certain ends to gain in having the Earl overthrown."

Myles bowed. "Sir," said he, "perhaps your ends are as much beyond anything that I can comprehend as though I were a little child, only this I know, that they must be very great. Ye know well that in any case I would fight this battle for my father's sake and for the honor of my house. Nevertheless, in return for all that it will so greatly advantage you, will ye not grant me a boon in return should I overcome my enemy?"

"What is your boon, Sir Myles?"

"That ye will grant me the favor to seek the Lady Alice de Mowbray for my wife."

The Earl of Mackworth started up from his seat. "Sir Myles Falworth"—he began violently, and then stopped short, drawing his bushy eyebrows together into a frown, stern, if not sinister.

Myles withstood his look calmly and impassively, and presently the Earl turned on his heel and strode to the open window. A long time passed in silence while he stood there, gazing out of the window into the garden beyond with his back to the young man.

Suddenly he swung around again. "Sir Myles," said he, "the family of Falworth is as good as any in Derbyshire. Just now it is poor and fallen in estate, but if it is again placed in credit and honor, ye, who are the son of the house, shall have your suit weighed with as much respect and consideration as though ye were my peer in all things. Such is my answer. Are ye satisfied?"

"I could ask no more," answered Myles.

CHAPTER · 29

THAT NIGHT Myles lodged at Mackworth House. The next morning, as soon as he had broken his fast, which he did in the privacy of his own apartments, the Earl bade him and Gascoyne make ready for the barge, which was then waiting at the river stairs to take them to Scotland Yard.

The Earl himself accompanied them, and as the heavy, snub-nosed boat, rowed by the six oarsmen in Mackworth livery, slid slowly and heavily up against the stream, the Earl, leaning back in his cushioned seat, pointed out the various houses of the great priests or nobles, palatial town residences standing mostly a little distance back from the water behind terraced high-walled gardens and lawns. Yonder was the Bishop of Exeter's close, yonder the Bishop of Bath's; that was York House, and that Chester Inn. So, passing by gardens and lawns and palaces, they came at last to Scotland Yard stairs, a broad flight of marble steps that led to a stone platform above, upon which opened the gateway to the garden beyond.

The Scotland Yard of Myles Falworth's day was one of the more pretentious and commodious of the palaces of the Strand. It took its name from having been from ancient times the London inn which the tributary kings of Scotland occupied when on their periodical visits of homage to England. Now, during this time of Scotland's independence, the Prince of Wales had taken up his lodging in the old palace, and made it noisy with the mad, boisterous mirth of his court.

As the watermen drew the barge close to the landing place of the stairs, the Earl stepped ashore. Followed by Myles and Gascoyne, he ascended to the broad gateway of the river wall of the garden. Three men-at-arms who lounged upon a bench under the shade of the little pentroof of a guardhouse beside the wall arose and saluted as the well-known figure of the Earl mounted the steps. The Earl nodded a cool answer. Passing unchallenged through the gate, he led the way up a pleached walk, beyond which, as Myles could see, there stretched a little grassy lawn and a stone-paved terrace. As the Earl and the two young men approached the end of the walk, they were met by the sound of voices and laughter, the clinking of glasses, and the rattle of dishes. Turning a corner, they came suddenly upon a party of young gentlemen, who sat at a late breakfast under the shade of a wide-spreading lime tree. They had evidently just left the tiltyard, for two of the guests— sturdy, thickset young knights—still wore a part of their tilting armor.

Behind the merry scene stood the gray, hoary old palace, a steep flight of stone steps, and a long, open, stone-arched gallery, which evidently led to the kitchen beyond, for along it hurried servingmen, running up and down the tall flight of steps, bearing trays and dishes and cups and flagons. It was a merry sight and a pleasant one. The day was warm and balmy, and the yellow sunlight fell in waving, uncertain patches of light, dappling the tablecloth and twinkling and sparkling upon the dishes, cups, and flagons.

At the head of the table sat a young man some three or four years older than Myles, dressed in a full suit of rich blue brocaded velvet, embroidered with gold thread and trimmed with black fur. His face, which was turned toward them as they mounted from the lawn to the little stone-flagged terrace, was frank and open, the cheeks smooth and fair, the eyes dark and blue. He was tall and rather slight, and wore his thick yellow hair hanging to his shoulders, where it was cut square across, after the manner of the times. Myles did not need to be told that this was the Prince of Wales.

"Ho, Gaffer Fox!" he cried, as soon as he caught sight of the Earl of Mackworth. "What wind blows you hither among us wild mallard drakes? I warrant it is not for love of us, but only to fill your own larder after the manner of Sir Fox among the drakes. Who is with you? Some gosling ye are about to pluck?"

A sudden hush fell upon the company, and all faces were turned toward the visitors.

The Earl bowed with a soft smile. "Your Highness," said he smoothly, "is pleased to be pleasant. Sir, I bring you the young knight of whom I spoke to you some time since—Sir Myles Falworth. You may be pleased to bring to mind that you so condescended as to promise to take him into your service until the fitting time arrived for that certain matter of which we spoke."

"Sir Myles," said the Prince of Wales, with a frank, pleasant smile, "I have heard great reports of your skill and prowess in France, both from Mackworth and from others. It will pleasure me greatly to have you in my household. More especially," he added, "as it will get you, callow as ye are, out of my Lord Fox's clutches. Our faction cannot do without the Earl of Mackworth's cunning wits, Sir Myles. Nevertheless I would not like to put all my fate and fortune into his hands without bond. I hope that ye do not rest your fortunes entirely upon his aid and countenance."

All who were present felt the discomfort of the Prince's speech. It was evident that one of his mad, wild humors was upon him. In another case the harebrained young courtiers around might have taken their cue from him, but the Earl of Mackworth was no subject for their gibes and witticisms. A constrained silence fell, in which the Earl alone maintained a perfect ease of manner.

Myles bowed to hide his own embarrassment. "Your Highness," said he, evasively, "I rest my fortune, first of all, upon God, His strength and justice."

"Ye will find safer dependence there than upon the Lord of Mackworth," said the Prince, dryly. "But come," he added, with a sudden change of voice and manner, "these be jests that border too closely upon bitter earnest for a merry breakfast. It is ill to idle with edged tools. Will ye not stay and break your fast with us, my lord?"

"Pardon me, your Highness," said the Earl, bowing, and smiling the same smooth smile his lips had worn from the first—such a smile as Myles had never thought to have seen upon his haughty face. "I crave your good leave to decline. I must return home presently, for your uncle, his Grace of Winchester, is awaiting my coming upon the business you know of. No doubt your Highness will find more joyance in a lusty young knight like Sir Myles than in an old fox like myself. So I leave him with you, in your good care."

Such was Myles' introduction to the wild young madcap Prince of Wales, afterward the famous Henry V, the conqueror of France.

For a month or more thereafter he was a member of the princely household, and, after a little while, a trusted and honored member. Perhaps it was the calm, sturdy strength, the courage of the young knight, that first appealed to the Prince's royal heart. Perhaps afterward it was the more sterling qualities that underlaid that courage that drew him to the young man. Certain it was that in two weeks Myles was the acknowledged favorite. He made no protestation of virtue. He always accompanied the Prince in those madcap ventures to London, where he beheld all manner of wild revelry. He never held himself aloof from his gay comrades, but he looked upon all their mad sports with the same calm gaze that had carried him without taint through the courts of Burgundy and the Dauphin. The gay, roistering young lords and gentlemen dubbed him Saint Myles, and jested with him about haircloth shirts and flagellations, but witticism and jest alike failed to move Myles' patient virtue. He went his own gait in the habits of his life, and in so going knew as little as the others of the mad court that the

Prince's growing liking for him was, perhaps more than all else, on account of that very temperance.

Then, by and by, the Prince began to confide in him as he did in none of the others. There was no great love between the King and his son. It has happened very often that the kings of England have felt bitter jealousy toward the heirs apparent as they have grown in power, and such was the case with the great King Henry IV. The Prince often spoke to Myles of the clashing and jarring between himself and his father, and the thought began to come to Myles' mind by degrees that maybe the King's jealousy accounted not a little for the Prince's reckless intemperance.

Once, for example, as the Prince leaned upon his shoulder waiting, while the attendants made ready the barge that was to carry them down the river to the city, he said, abruptly: "Myles, what think ye of us all? Does not your honesty hold us in contempt?"

"Nay, Highness," said Myles. "How could I hold contempt?"

"Marry," said the Prince, "I myself hold contempt, and am not as honest a man as ye. But, prithee, have patience with me, Myles. Someday, perhaps, I too will live a clean life. Now, if I live seriously, the King will be more jealous of me than ever, and that is not a little. Maybe I live thus so that he may not know what I really am."

The Prince also often talked to Myles concerning his own affairs: of the battle he was to fight for his father's honor, of how the Earl of

Mackworth had plotted and planned to bring him face to face with the Earl of Alban. He spoke to Myles more than once of the many great changes of state and party that hung upon the downfall of the enemy of the house of Falworth, and showed him how no hand but his own could strike that enemy down; if he fell, it must be through the son of Falworth. Sometimes it seemed to Myles as though he and his blind father were the center of a great web of plot and intrigue, stretching far and wide, that included not only the greatest houses of England, but royalty and the political balance of the country as well. Even before the greatness of it all he did not flinch.

Then, at last, came the beginning of the time for action. It was in the early part of May, and Myles had been a member of the Prince's household for a little over a month. One morning he was ordered to attend the Prince in his privy cabinet. Obeying the summons, he found the Prince, his younger brother, the Duke of Bedford, and his uncle, the Bishop of Winchester, seated at a table, where they had just been refreshing themselves with wine and wafers.

"My poor Myles," said the Prince, smiling, as the young knight bowed to the three, and then stood erect, as though on duty. "It shames my heart, brother—and ye, uncle—it shames my heart to be one privy to this thing which we are set upon to do. Here be we, the greatest lords of England, making a cat's-paw of this lad—for he is only yet a boy—and of his blind father, to achieve our ends against Alban's faction. It seems not overhonorable to my mind."

"Pardon me, your Highness," said Myles, blushing to the roots of his hair, "but if I may be so bold as to speak, I know nothing of what your aims may be. I only look to restoring my father's honor and the honor of our house."

"Truly," said the Prince, smiling, "that is the only matter that makes me willing to lay my hands to this business. Do ye know why I have sent for you? It is because this day ye must challenge the Duke of Alban before the King. The Earl of Mackworth has laid all his plans and the time is now ripe. Do you know that your father is at Mackworth House?"

"Nay," said Myles. "I knew it not."

"He has been there for nearly two days," said the Prince. "Just now the Earl has sent for us to come first to Mackworth House, then to go to the palace, for he has gained audience with the King, and has so arranged it that the Earl of Alban is to be there as well. We all go straightway. So get yourself ready as soon as possible."

Perhaps Myles' heart began beating more quickly within him at the nearness of that great happening which he had looked forward to for so long. If it did, he made no sign of his emotion, but only asked, "How must I clothe myself, your Highness?"

"Wear your light armor," said the Prince, "but no helmet, a tunic bearing the arms and colors that the Earl gave you when ye were knighted, and carry your right-hand gauntlet under your belt for your challenge. Now make haste, for time passes."

CHAPTER · 30

ADJOINING THE ANCIENT PALACE of Westminster, where King Henry IV was then holding his court, was a no less ancient stone building known as the Painted Room. Upon the walls were depicted a series of battle scenes in long bands reaching around the room, one above another. Some of the pictures had been painted as far back as the days of Henry III, others had been added since his time. They chronicled the various wars of the kings of England, and it was from them that the little hall took its name of the Painted Room.

This ancient wing, or offshoot, of the main building was more retired from the hurly-burly of outer life than other parts of the palace, and thither the sick King was very fond of retiring from the business of state—which ever rested more and more heavily upon his shoulders—sometimes to squander in quietness a spare hour or two; sometimes to idle over a favorite book; sometimes to play a game of chess with a favorite courtier. The cold painted walls had been hung with tapestry, and the floor had been spread with arras carpet. These and the cushioned couches and chairs that stood around gave its gloomy antiquity an air of comfort—an air even of luxury.

It was to this favorite retreat of the King's that Myles was brought that morning with his father to face the great Earl of Alban.

In the anteroom the little party of princes and nobles who escorted the father and son had held a brief consultation. Then the others had entered, leaving Myles and his blind father in charge of Lord Lumley and two knights of the court, Sir Reginald Hallowell and Sir Piers Averell.

Myles, as he stood patiently waiting, with his father's arm resting in his, could hear the muffled sound of voices from beyond the curtain. Among others he recognized the well-remembered tones of the King. He fancied that he heard his own name mentioned more than once, and then the sound of talking ceased. The next moment the curtain was drawn aside, and the Earl entered the antechamber again.

"All is ready, cousin," said he to Lord Falworth, in a suppressed voice. "Essex has done as he promised, and Alban is within there now." Then, turning to Myles, speaking in the same low voice, and betraying more agitation than Myles had thought it possible for him to show. "Sir Myles," said he, "remember all that has been told you. Ye know what ye have to say and do." Then, without further word, he took Lord Falworth by the hand and led the way into the room, Myles following close behind.

The King half sat, half reclined, upon a cushioned seat close to which stood the two princes. There were some dozen others present, mostly priests and noblemen of high degree who clustered in a group at a little distance. Myles knew most of them at a glance, having seen them come and go at Scotland Yard. But among them all he singled out only one—the Earl of Alban. He had not seen that face since he was a little child eight years old, but now that he beheld it again, it fitted instantly and vividly into the remembrance of the time of that terrible scene at Falworth Castle, when he had beheld the then Lord Brookhurst standing above the dead body of Sir John Dale, with the bloody mace clenched in his hand. There were the same heavy black brows, sinister and gloomy, the same hooked nose, the same swarthy cheeks. He even remembered the deep dent in the forehead, where the brows met in perpetual frown. So it was that upon that face his looks centered and rested.

The Earl of Alban had just been speaking to some lord who stood beside him, and a half-smile still hung about the corners of his lips. At first, as he looked up at the entrance of the newcomers, there was no other expression. Suddenly came a flash of recognition, a look of wide-eyed amazement. Then the blood left the cheeks and the lips, and the face grew very pale. No doubt he saw at a flash that some great danger overhung him in this sudden coming of his old enemy, for he was as keen and as astute a politician as he was a famous warrior. At least he knew that the eyes of most of those present were fixed keenly and searchingly upon him. After the first start of recognition, his left hand, hanging at his side, gradually closed around the scabbard of his sword, clutching it in a viselike grip.

Meantime the Earl of Mackworth had led the blind lord to the King, where both kneeled.

"Why, how now, my lord?" said the King. "I thought it was our young Paladin whom we knighted at Devlen that was to be presented, and here ye bring this old man. A blind man, ha! What is the meaning of this?"

"Majesty," said the Earl, "I have taken this chance to bring to your merciful consideration one who has most woefully and unjustly suffered from your anger. Yonder stands the young knight of whom we spoke. This is his father, Gilbert Reginald, formerly Lord Falworth, who craves mercy and justice at your hands."

"Falworth," said the King, placing his hand to his head. "The name is not strange to my ears, but I cannot place it. My head has troubled me sorely today, and I cannot remember."

At this point the Earl of Alban came quietly and deliberately forward. "Sire," said he, "pardon my boldness in so venturing to address you, but I can bring the name more clearly to your mind. He is, as my Lord of Mackworth said, the former Lord Falworth, the outlawed, attainted traitor; so declared for the harboring of Sir John Dale, who was one of those who sought your Majesty's life at Windsor eleven years ago. Sire, he is my enemy as well, and is brought hither by my proclaimed enemies. Should anything occur to my harm, I rest my case in your gracious hands."

The dusky red flamed into the King's pale, sickly face in answer, and he rose hastily from his seat.

"Aye," said he, "I remember now—I remember the man and the name! Who has dared bring him here before us?" All the dull heaviness of sickness was gone for the moment, and King Henry was the King Henry of ten years ago as he rolled his eyes balefully from one to another of the courtiers who stood silently around.

The Earl of Mackworth shot a covert glance at the Bishop of Winchester, who came forward in answer.

"Your Majesty," said he, "here am I, your brother, who beseech you as your brother not to judge overhastily in this matter. It is true that this man has been adjudged a traitor, but he has been so adjudged without a hearing. I beseech you to listen patiently to whatsoever he may have to say."

The King fixed the Bishop with a look of the bitterest, deepest anger, holding his nether lip tightly under his teeth—a trick he had when strongly moved with anger—and the Bishop's eyes fell under the look. Meantime the Earl of Alban stood calm and silent. No doubt he saw that the King's anger was likely to befriend him more than any words that he himself could say, and he endangered his case with no more speech which could only prove superfluous.

At last the King turned a face red and swollen

with anger to the blind lord, who still kneeled before him.

"What have ye to say?" he said, in a deep and sullen voice.

"Gracious and merciful lord," said the blind nobleman, "I come to you, the fountainhead of justice, craving justice. Sire, I do now and here deny my treason, which denial I could not before make, being blind and helpless, and my enemies strong and malignant. But now, sire, heaven has sent me help, and therefore I do acclaim before you that my accuser, William Bushy Brookhurst, Earl of Alban, is a foul and an attainted liar in all that he has accused me of. To uphold which allegation, and to defend me, who am blinded by his unknightliness, I do offer a champion to prove all that I say with his body in combat."

The Earl of Mackworth darted a quick look at Myles, who came forward the moment his father had ended, and kneeled beside him. The King offered no interruption to his speech, but he bent a look heavy with anger upon the young man.

"My gracious lord and king," said Myles, "I, the son of the accused, do offer myself as his champion in this cause, beseeching you of your grace leave to prove the truth of the same, being a belted knight by your grace and of your creation, and the peer of any who wears spurs." Thereupon, rising, he drew his iron gauntlet from his girdle and flung it clashing down upon the floor. With his heart swelling with anger and indignation and pity of his blind father, he cried in a loud voice, "I do accuse you, William of Alban, that ye lie vilely as aforesaid, and here cast down my gage, daring you to take it up."

The Earl of Alban made as though he would accept the challenge, but the King stopped him hastily.

"Stop!" he cried, harshly. "Touch not the gage! Let it lie—let it lie, I tell you, my lord! Now then," said he, turning to the others, "tell me what means all this confusion? Who brought this man hither?"

He looked from one to another of those who stood silently around, but no one answered.

"I see," said he. "Ye all have had to do with it. It is as my Lord Alban says. Ye are his enemies, and ye are my enemies as well. In this I do smell a vile plot. I cannot undo what I have done, and since I have made this young man a knight with my own hands, I cannot deny that he is fit to challenge my Lord of Alban. Nevertheless, the High Court of Chivalry shall adjudge this case. Meantime," said he, turning to the Earl Marshal, who was present, "I give you this attainted lord in charge. Convey him presently to the Tower, and let him abide our pleasure there. Also, ye may take up yon gage, and keep it till it is redeemed according to our pleasure."

He stood thoughtfully for a moment, and then, raising his eyes, looked fixedly at the Earl of Mackworth.

"I know," he said, "that I am a right sick man, and there are some who are already plotting to overthrow those who have held up my hand with their own strength for all these years."

Then speaking more directly: "My Lord Earl of Mackworth, I see your hand in this before all others. It was ye who so played upon me as to get me to knight this young man, and thus make him worthy to challenge my Lord of Alban. It was your doing that brought him here today, backed by my own sons and my brother and by these noblemen." Then turning suddenly to the Earl of Alban: "Come, my lord," said he; "I am weary with all this confusion. Lend me your arm to leave this place." So it was that he left the room, leaning upon the Earl of Alban's arm, and followed by the two or three of the Alban faction who were present.

"Your Royal Highness," said the Earl Marshal, "I must do the King's bidding, and take this gentleman into arrest."

"Do your duty," said the Prince. "We knew it must come to this. Meanwhile he is to be a prisoner of honor, and see that he be well lodged and cared for. Ye will find my barge at the stairs to convey him down the river, and I myself will come this afternoon to visit him."

CHAPTER · 31

IT WAS NOT UNTIL the end of July that the High Court of Chivalry rendered its judgment. There were many unusual points in the case, some of which bore heavily against Lord Falworth, some of which were in his favor. He was very ably defended by the lawyers whom the Earl of Mackworth had engaged upon his side. Nevertheless, under ordinary circumstances the judgment, no doubt, would have been quickly rendered against him. As it was, however, the circumstances were not ordinary, and it was rendered in his favor. The Court besought the King to grant the ordeal by battle, to accept Lord Falworth's champion, and to appoint the time and place for the meeting.

The decision must have been a most bitter, galling one for the sick King. He was naturally of a generous, forgiving nature, but Lord Falworth in his time of power had been an unrelenting and fearless opponent, and his Majesty, who, like most generous men, could on occasion be very cruel and intolerant, had never forgiven him. He had steadily thrown the might of his influence with the Court against the Falworths' case, but that influence was no longer all-powerful for good or ill. He was failing in health, and it could be a matter of only a few years, probably of only a few months, before his successor sat upon the throne.

On the other hand, the Prince of Wales' faction had been steadily, and of late rapidly, increasing in power; and in the Earl of Mackworth, its virtual head, it possessed one of the most capable politicians and astute intriguers in Europe. So, as the outcome of all the plotting and counterplotting, scheming and counterscheming, the case was decided in Lord Falworth's favor. The knowledge of the ultimate result was known to the Prince of Wales' circle almost a week before it was finally decided. Indeed, the Earl of Mackworth had made pretty sure of that result before he had summoned Myles from France, but upon the King it fell like the shock of a sudden blow. All that day he kept himself in moody seclusion, nursing his silent, bitter anger, and making only one outbreak, in which he swore by the Holy Rood that should Myles be worsted in the encounter, he would not take the battle into his own hands, but would suffer him to be slain; and, furthermore, that should the Earl show signs of failing at any time, he would do all in his power to save him. One of the courtiers who had been present, and who was secretly inclined to the Prince of Wales' faction, had repeated this speech at Scotland Yard, and the Prince had said:

"That means, Myles, that ye must either win or die."

"And so I would have it, my lord," Myles had answered.

It was not until nearly a fortnight after the decision of the Court of Chivalry had been rendered that the King announced the time and place of battle—the time to be the third of September, the place to be Smithfield—a spot much used for such encounters.

During the three weeks or so that intervened between this announcement and the time of combat, Myles went nearly every day to visit the lists in course of erection. Often the Prince went with him. Always two or three of his friends of the Scotland Yard court accompanied him.

The lists were laid out in the usual form. The true or principal list in which the combatants were to engage was sixty yards long and forty yards wide. This rectangular space was surrounded by a fence about six feet high, painted vermilion. Between the fence and the stand where the King and the spectators sat, and surrounding the central space, was the outer or false list, also surrounded by a fence. In the false list the constable and the marshal and their followers and attendants were to be stationed at the time of battle to preserve the general peace during the contest between the principals.

One day as Myles, his princely patron, and his friends entered the barriers, leaving their horses at the outer gate, they met the Earl of Alban and his followers, who were just quitting the lists, which they also were in the habit of visiting nearly every day. As the two parties passed one another, the Earl spoke to a gentleman walking beside him and in a voice loud enough to be clearly overheard by the others:

"Yonder is the young sprig of Falworth," said he. "His father, my lords, is not content with forfeiting his own life for his treason, but must throw away his son's also. I have faced and overthrown many a better knight than that boy."

Myles heard the speech, and knew that it was intended for him to hear, but he paid no attention, walking composedly at the Prince's side. The Prince had also overheard it, and after a little space of silence asked:

"Do ye not feel anxiety for your coming battle, Myles?"

"Yeah, my lord," said Myles; "sometimes I do feel anxiety, but not such as my Lord of Alban would have me feel in uttering that speech. It is anxiety for my father's sake and mother's sake that I feel, for truly there are great matters for them pending upon this fight. Nevertheless, I do know that God will not desert me in my cause, for verily my father is no traitor."

"But the Earl of Alban," said the Prince, gravely, "is reputed one of the best-skilled knights in all England. Moreover, he is merciless and without generosity, so that if he gains advantage over you, he will surely slay you."

"I am not afraid, my lord," said Myles, still calmly and composedly.

"Nor am I afraid for you, Myles," said the Prince heartily, putting his arm around the young man's shoulder; "for truly, were ye a knight of forty years, instead of one of twenty, ye could not bear yourself with more courage."

As the time for the duel approached, the days seemed to drag themselves along on leaden feet. Nevertheless, the days came and went, as all days do, bringing with them, at last, the fateful third of September.

Early in the morning, while the sun was still level and red, the Prince himself, unattended, came to Myles' apartment, in the outer room of which Gascoyne was bustling busily about arranging the armor piece by piece, renewing straps and thongs, but not whistling over his work as he usually did. The Prince nodded to him, and then passed silently through to the inner chamber. Myles was upon his knees, and Father Ambrose, the Prince's chaplain, was beside him. The Prince stood silently at the door, until Myles, having told his last bead, rose and turned toward him.

"My dear lord," said the young knight, "I give you gramercy for the great honor you do me in coming so early to visit me."

"Nay, Myles, give me no thanks," said the Prince, frankly reaching him his hand, which Myles took and set to his lips. "I lay thinking me of you this morning, while yet in bed, and so, as I could not sleep any more, I was moved to come hither to see you."

Quite a number of the Prince's faction were at the breakfast at Scotland Yard that morning; among others, the Earl of Mackworth. All were more or less oppressed with anxiety, for nearly all of them had staked much upon the coming battle. If Alban conquered, he would be more powerful to harm them and to avenge himself upon them than ever, and Myles was a very young champion upon whom to depend. Myles himself showed as little anxiety, perhaps, as any. He certainly ate more heartily of his breakfast that morning than many of the others.

After the meal was ended, the Prince rose.

"The boat is ready at the stairs," said he; "if ye would go to the Tower to visit your father, Myles, before hearing mass, I and Cholmondeley and Vere and Poins will go with you, if ye, lords and gentlemen, will grant me your pardon for leaving you. Are there any others that ye would have accompany you?"

"I would have Sir James Lee and my squire, Master Gascoyne, if ye are so pleased to give them leave to go," answered Myles.

"So be it," said the Prince. "We will stop at Mackworth stairs for the knight."

The barge landed at the west stairs of the

Tower wharf, and the whole party was received with more than usual civilities by the governor, who conducted them at once to the Tower, where Lord Falworth lodged. Lady Falworth met them at the head of the stairs. Her eyes were very red and her face pale, and as Myles raised her hand and set a long kiss upon it, her lips trembled, and she turned her face away quickly, pressing her handkerchief for one moment to her eyes. Poor lady! What agony of anxiety and dread did she not suffer for her boy's sake that day! Myles had not hidden from her or his father that he must either win or die.

As Myles turned from his mother, Prior Edward came out from the inner chamber and was greeted warmly by him. The old priest had arrived in London only the day before, having come down from Crosbey Priory to be with his friend's family in this time of terrible anxiety.

After a little while of general talk, the Prince and his attendants retired, leaving the family together, only Sir James Lee and Gascoyne remaining behind.

Many matters that had been discussed before were now finally settled, the chief of which was the disposition of Lady Falworth in case the battle should go against them. Then Myles took his leave, kissing his mother, who began crying, and comforting her with brave assurances. Prior Edward accompanied him as far as the head of the Tower stairs, where Myles kneeled on the stone steps, while the good priest blessed him and signed the cross upon his forehead. The Prince was waiting in the walled garden adjoining, and as they rowed back again up the river to Scotland Yard, all were thoughtful and serious, even Poins' and Vere's merry tongues being stilled from their usual quips and jesting.

It was about the quarter of the hour before eleven o'clock when Myles, with Gascoyne, set forth for the lists. The Prince of Wales, together with most of his court, had already gone on to Smithfield, leaving behind him six young knights of his household to act as escort to the young champion. Then at last the order to horse was given. The great gate swung open, and out they rode, clattering and jingling, the sunlight gleaming and flaming and flashing upon their polished armor. They drew rein to the right, and so rode in a little cloud of dust along the Strand Street toward London town, with the breeze blowing merrily and the sunlight shining as sweetly and blithesomely as though they were riding to a wedding rather than to a grim and dreadful ordeal that meant either victory or death.

CHAPTER · 32

IN THE DAYS of King Edward III a code of laws relating to trial by battle had been compiled for one of his sons, Thomas of Woodstock. In this work each and every detail, to the most minute, had been arranged and fixed, and from that time judicial combats had been regulated in accordance with its mandates.

It was in obedience to this code that Myles

Falworth appeared at the east gate of the lists (the east gate being assigned by law to the challenger), clad in full armor of proof, attended by Gascoyne, and accompanied by two of the young knights who had acted as his escort from Scotland Yard.

At the barrier he was met by the attorney Willingwood, the chief lawyer who had conducted the Falworth case before the High Court of Chivalry, and who was to attend him during the administration of the oaths before the King.

As Myles presented himself at the gate he was met by the constable, the marshal, and their immediate attendants. The constable, laying his hand upon the bridle rein, said in a loud voice: "Stand, Sir Knight, and tell me why ye come thus armed to the gates of the lists. What is your name? Wherefore do ye come?"

Myles answered, "I am Myles Falworth, a Knight of the Bath by grace of his Majesty King Henry IV and by his creation, and do come hither to defend my challenge upon the body of William Bushy Brookhurst, Earl of Alban, proclaiming him an unknightly knight and a false and perjured liar, in that he has accused Gilbert Reginald, Lord Falworth, of treason against our beloved lord, his Majesty the King, and may God defend the right!"

As he ended speaking, the constable advanced close to his side, and formally raising the visor of the helmet, looked him in the face. Thereupon, having approved his identity, he ordered the gates to be opened, and bade Myles enter the lists with his squire and his friends.

At the south side of the lists a raised scaffolding had been built for the King and those who looked on. It was not unlike that which had been erected at Devlen Castle when Myles had first jousted as belted knight—here were the same raised seat for the King, the tapestries, the hangings, the fluttering pennons, and the royal standard floating above. Only here were no fair-faced ladies looking down upon him, but, instead, stern-browed lords and knights in armor, and squires. Here were no merry laughing and buzz of talk and flutter of fans and kerchiefs, but all was very quiet and serious.

Myles riding upon his horse, with Gascoyne holding the bridle rein and his attorney walking beside him with his hand upon the stirrups, followed the constable across the lists to an open space in front of the seat where the King sat. Then, having reached his appointed station, he stopped, and the constable, advancing to the foot of the stairway that led to the dais above, announced in a loud voice that the challenger had entered the lists.

"Then call the defendant straightway," said the King, "for noon draws nigh."

The day was very warm, and the sun, bright and unclouded, shone fiercely down upon the open lists. Perhaps few men nowadays could bear the scorching heat of iron plates such as Myles wore, from which the body was protected only by a leather jacket and hose. But men's bodies in those days were tougher and more seasoned to hardships of weather than they are in our times. Myles thought no more of the burning iron plates that encased him than a modern soldier thinks of his dress uniform in warm weather. Nevertheless, he raised the visor of his helmet to cool his face as he waited the coming of his opponent. He turned his eyes upward to the row of seats on the scaffolding above, and even in the restless, bewildering multitude of strange faces turned toward him he recognized those that he knew: the Prince of Wales, his companions of the Scotland Yard household, the Duke of Clarence, the Bishop of Winchester, and some of the noblemen of the Earl of Mackworth's party who had been buzzing about the Prince for the past month or so. But his glance swept over all these, rather perceiving than seeing them, and then rested upon a square boxlike compartment not unlike a prisoner's dock in the courtroom of our day, for in the box sat his father, with the Earl of Mackworth upon one side and Sir James Lee upon the other. The blind man's face was very pale, but still wore its usual expression of calm serenity— the calm serenity of a blind face. The Earl was also very pale, and he kept his eyes fixed steadfastly upon Myles with a keen and searching look, as though to pierce to the very bottom of the young man's heart and discover if indeed not one little fragment of fear or uncertainty tainted the solid courage of his knighthood.

Then he heard the criers calling the defendant at the four corners of the list: "Oyez! Oyez! Oyez! William Bushy Brookhurst, Earl of Alban, come to this combat, in which you be enterprised this day to discharge your sureties before the King, the constable, and the marshal, and to encounter in your defense Myles Falworth, knight, the accepted champion upon behalf of Gilbert

Reginald Falworth, the challenger! Oyez! Oyez! Oyez! Let the defendant come!"

So they continued calling, until, by the sudden turning of all faces, Myles knew that his enemy was at hand.

Then presently he saw the Earl and his attendants enter the outer gate at the west end of the barrier. He saw the constable and marshal meet him. He saw the formal words of greeting pass. He saw the constable raise the visor of the helmet. Then the gate opened, and the Earl of Alban entered, clad head to foot in a full suit of magnificent Milan armor without tunic or adornment of any kind. As he approached across the lists, Myles closed the visor of his helmet, and then sat quite still and motionless, for the time was come.

So he sat, erect and motionless as a statue of iron, half hearing the reading of the long, intricately worded bills, absorbed in many thoughts of past and present things. At last the reading ended, and then he calmly and composedly obeyed, under the direction of his attorney, the several forms and ceremonies that followed, answered the various official questions, took the various oaths. Then Gascoyne, leading the horse by the bridle rein, conducted him back to his station at the east end of the lists.

As the faithful friend and squire made one last and searching examination of arms and armor, the marshal and clerk came to the young champion and administered the oath by which he swore that he carried no concealed weapons.

The weapons allowed by the High Court were then measured and attested. They consisted of the long sword, the short sword, the dagger, the mace, and a weapon known as the hand gisarm, or glavelot—a heavy, swordlike blade eight palms long, a palm in breadth, and riveted to a stout handle of wood three feet long.

The usual lance had not been included in the list of arms, the hand gisarm being substituted in its place. It was a fearful and murderous weapon, though cumbersome, unhandy, and ill adapted for quick or dexterous stroke. Nevertheless, the Earl of Alban had petitioned the King to have it included in the list, and in answer to the King's expressed desire the Court had adopted it in place of the lance, yielding this much to the royal wishes. Nor was it a small concession. The hand gisarm had been a weapon very much in vogue in King Richard's day, and was now nearly, if not entirely, out of fashion with the younger generation of warriors. The Earl of Alban was, of course, well used to the blade. With Myles it was strange and new, either for attack or in defense.

With the administration of the final oath and the examination of the weapons, the preliminary ceremonies came to an end, and presently Myles heard the criers calling to clear the lists. As those around him moved to withdraw, the young knight drew off his mailed gauntlet, and gave Gascoyne's hand one last final clasp, strong, earnest, and intense with the close friendship of young manhood. Poor Gascoyne looked up at him with a face ghastly white.

Then all were gone; the gates of the principal list and that of the false list were closed clash-

ing, and Myles was alone, face to face with his
mortal enemy.

CHAPTER · 33

THERE WAS A LITTLE TIME of restless, rustling silence, during which the constable took his place
in the seat appointed for him directly in front
of and below the King's throne. A moment or
two when even the restlessness and the rustling
were quieted, and then the King leaned forward and spoke to the constable, who immediately called out, in a loud, clear voice:

"Let them go!" Then again: "Let them go!"
Then, for the third and last time: "Let them go
and do their endeavor, in God's name!"

At this third command the combatants,
each of whom had till that moment been sitting
as motionless as a statue of iron, tightened rein,
and rode slowly and deliberately forward without haste, yet without hesitation, until they met
in the very middle of the lists.

In the battle which followed, Myles fought
with the long sword, the Earl with the hand
gisarm for which he had asked. The moment
they met, the combat was opened, and for a time
nothing was heard but the thunderous clashing
and clamor of blows, now and then rising with
a ceaseless uproar and din, now and then beating intermittently, now and then pausing. Occasionally, as the combatants spurred together,
checked, wheeled, and recovered, they would
be hidden for a moment in a misty veil of dust,

which, again drifting down the wind, perhaps revealed them drawn a little apart, resting their panting horses. Then, again, they would spur together, striking as they passed, wheeling, and striking again.

Upon the scaffolding all was still, except now and then for the buzz of muffled exclamations or applause of those who looked on. Mostly the applause was from Myles' friends, for from the very first he showed and steadily maintained his advantage over the older man. "Hah! well struck! well recovered!" "Look ye! the sword bit that time!" "Nay, look, saw ye him pass the point of the gisarm?" Then, "Falworth! Falworth!" as some more than usually skillful stroke or parry occurred.

Meantime Myles' father sat straining his sightless eyeballs, as though to pierce his body's darkness with one ray of light that would show him how his boy held his own in the fight, and Lord Mackworth, leaning with his lips close to the blind man's ear, told him point by point how the battle stood.

"Fear not, Gilbert," said he at each pause in the fight. "He holds his own right well." Then, after a while: "God is with us, Gilbert. Alban is twice wounded and his horse fails. One little while longer and the victory is ours!"

A longer and more continuous interval of combat followed this last assurance, during which Myles drove the assault fiercely and relentlessly, as though to overbear his enemy by the very power and violence of the blows he delivered. The Earl defended himself desperately, but was borne back, back, back, farther and farther. Every nerve of those who looked on was stretched to breathless tenseness, when, almost as his enemy was against the barriers, Myles paused and rested.

"Out upon it!" exclaimed the Earl of Mackworth, almost shrill in his excitement, as the sudden lull followed the crashing of blows. "Why does the boy spare him? That is thrice he has given him grace to recover. If he had pushed the battle he would have driven him back against the barriers."

It was as the Earl had said. Myles three times had given his enemy grace when victory was almost in his very grasp. He had three times spared him, in spite of all he and those dear to him must suffer should his cruel and merciless enemy gain the victory. It was a false and foolish generosity, partly the fault of his impulsive youth—more largely of his romantic training in the artificial code of French chivalry. He felt that the battle was his, and so he gave his enemy these three chances to recover, as some chevalier or knight-errant of romance might have done, instead of pushing the combat to a mercifully speedy end—and his foolish generosity cost him dear.

In the momentary pause that had thus stirred the Earl of Mackworth to a sudden outbreak, the Earl of Alban sat upon his panting, sweating war horse, facing his powerful young enemy at about twelve paces distant. He sat as still as a rock, holding his gisarm poised in front of him. He had, as the Earl of Mackworth had said, been wounded twice, and each time with the point of the sword, so much more dangerous than a direct cut with the weapon. One wound was beneath his armor, and no one but he knew how serious it might be. The other was under the overlapping of the épaulière, and from it a finger's breadth of blood ran straight down his side and over the housings of his horse. From without, the still, motionless iron figure appeared calm and expressionless. Within, who knows what blasts of hate, rage, and despair swept his heart as with a fiery whirlwind.

As Myles looked at the motionless, bleeding figure, his breast swelled with pity. "My lord," said he, "ye are sore wounded and the fight is against you. Will ye not yield?"

No one but that other heard the speech, and no one but Myles heard the answer that came back, hollow, cavernous, "Never, dog! Never!"

Then in an instant, as quick as a flash, his enemy spurred straight upon Myles, and as he spurred he struck a desperate, swinging blow, in which he threw in one final effort all the strength of hate, of fury, and of despair. Myles whirled his horse backward, warding the blow with his shield as he did so. The blade glanced from the smooth face of the shield, and, whether by mistake or not, fell straight and true, and with almost undiminished force, upon the neck of Myles' war horse, just behind the ears. The animal staggered forward, and then fell upon its knees, and at the same instant the other, as though by the impetus of the rush, dashed full upon it with all the momentum lent by the weight of iron it carried. The shock was irresistible, and the stunned and wounded horse was flung upon the ground, rolling over and over.

As his horse fell, Myles wrenched one of his feet out of the stirrup; the other caught for an instant, and he was flung headlong with stunning violence, his armor crashing as he fell. In the cloud of dust that arose no one could see just what happened, but that what was done was done deliberately no one doubted. The Earl, at once checking and spurring his foaming charger, drove the iron-shod war horse directly over Myles' prostrate body. Then, checking him fiercely with the curb, reined him back, the hoofs clashing and crashing over the figure beneath. So he had ridden over the father at York, and so he rode over the son at Smithfield.

Myles, as he lay prostrate and half stunned by his fall, had seen his enemy thus driving his rearing horse down upon him, but was not able to defend himself. A fallen knight in full armor was utterly powerless to rise without assistance; Myles lay helpless in the clutch of the very iron that was his defense. He closed his eyes involuntarily, and then horse and rider were upon him. There was a deafening, sparkling crash, a glimmering faintness, then another crash as the horse was reined furiously back again, and then a humming stillness.

In a moment, upon the scaffolding all was a tumult of uproar and confusion, shouting and gesticulation. Only the King sat calm, sullen, impassive. The Earl wheeled his horse and sat for a moment or two as though to make quite sure that he knew the King's mind. The blow that had been given was foul, unknightly, but the King gave no sign either of approbation or rebuke. He had willed that Myles was to die.

Then the Earl turned again, and rode deliberately up to his prostrate enemy.

When Myles opened his eyes after that moment of stunning silence, it was to see the other looming above him on his war horse, swinging his gisarm for one last mortal pitiless blow.

The sight of that looming peril brought back Myles' wandering senses like a flash of lightning. He flung up his shield, and met the blow even as it descended, turning it aside. It only protracted the end.

Once more the Earl of Alban raised the gisarm, swinging it twice around his head before he struck. This time, though the shield glanced it, the blow fell upon the shoulder piece, biting through the steel plate and leather jacket beneath even to the bone. Then Myles covered his head with his shield as a last protecting chance for life.

For the third time the Earl swung the blade flashing, and then it fell, straight and true, upon the defenseless body, just below the left arm, biting deep through the armor plates. For an instant the blade stuck fast, and that instant was Myles' salvation. Under the agony of the blow he gave a muffled cry, and almost instinctively grasped the shaft of the weapon with both hands. Had the Earl let go his end of the weapon, he would have won the battle at his leisure and most easily; as it was, he struggled violently to wrench the gisarm away from Myles. In that short, fierce struggle Myles was dragged to his knees, and then, still holding the weapon with one hand, he clutched the trappings of the Earl's horse with the other. The next moment he was

on his feet. The other struggled to thrust him away, but Myles, letting go the gisarm, which he held with his left hand, clutched him tightly by the sword belt in the intense, viselike grip of despair. In vain the Earl strove to beat him loose with the shaft of the gisarm, in vain he spurred and reared his horse to shake him off. Myles held him tight, in spite of his struggles.

He felt neither the streaming blood nor the throbbing agony of his wounds. Every faculty of soul, mind, body, every power of life, was centered in one intense, burning effort. He neither felt, thought, nor reasoned, but clutching, with the blindness of instinct the heavy, spiked, iron-headed mace that hung at the Earl's saddlebow, he gave it one tremendous wrench that snapped the plaited leather thongs that held it as though they were skeins of thread. Then, grinding his teeth as with a spasm, he struck as he had never struck before—once, twice, thrice full upon the front of the helmet. Crash! crash! And then, even as the Earl toppled sidelong, crash! The iron plates split and crackled under the third blow. Myles had one flashing glimpse of an awful face, and then the saddle was empty.

As he held tight to the horse, panting, dizzy, sick to death, he felt the hot blood gushing from his side, filling his body armor, and staining the ground upon which he stood. Still he held tightly to the saddlebow of the fallen man's horse until, through his glimmering sight, he saw the marshal, the lieutenant, and the attendants gather around him. He heard the marshal ask him, in a voice that sounded faint and distant, if he were dangerously wounded. He did not answer, and one of the attendants, leaping from his horse, opened the visor of his helmet, disclosing the dull, hollow eyes, the ashy, colorless lips, and the waxen forehead, upon which stood great beads of sweat.

"Water! water!" he cried, hoarsely; "give me water!" Then, quitting his hold upon the horse, he started blindly across the lists toward the gate of the barrier. A shadow that chilled his heart seemed to fall upon him. "It is death," he muttered. Then he stopped, swayed for an instant, then toppled headlong, crashing as he fell.

CHAPTER · 34

BUT MYLES WAS NOT DEAD. Those who had seen his face when the visor of the helmet was raised, and then saw him fall as he tottered across the lists, had at first thought so. But his faintness was more from loss of blood and the sudden unstringing of nerve and sense from the intense furious strain of the last few moments of battle than from the vital nature of the wound. Indeed, after Myles had been carried out of the lists and laid upon the ground in the shade between the barriers, Master Thomas, the Prince's barber surgeon, having examined the wound, declared that he might be even carried on a covered litter to Scotland Yard without serious danger. The Prince was extremely desirous of having him under his care, and so the venture was tried. Myles was carried to Scotland Yard, and perhaps was none the worse for it.

The Prince, the Earl of Mackworth, and two or three others stood silently watching as the worthy shaver and leecher, assisted by his apprentice and Gascoyne, washed and bathed the great gaping wound in the side, and bound it with linen bandages. Myles lay with closed eyelids, still, pallid, weak as a little child. Presently he opened his eyes and turned them, dull and languid, to the Prince.

"What has happened to my father, my lord?" said he, in a faint, whispering voice.

"Ye have saved his life and honor, Myles," the Prince answered. "He is here now, and your mother has been sent for, and comes soon with the priest who was with them this morning."

Myles dropped his eyelids again. His lips moved, but he made no sound, and then two bright tears trickled across his white cheek.

"He makes a woman of me," the Prince muttered through his teeth, and then, swinging on his heel, he stood for a long time looking out of the window into the garden beneath.

"May I see my father?" said Myles presently, without opening his eyes. The Prince turned around and looked inquiringly at the surgeon.

The good man shook his head. "Not today," said he; "perhaps tomorrow he may see him and his mother. The bleeding is but new stanched, and such matters as seeing his father and mother may make the heart swell, and so maybe the wound burst afresh and he die. If he would hope to live, he must rest quiet until tomorrow."

But though Myles' wound was not mortal, it

was very serious. The fever which followed lingered longer than common—perhaps because of the hot weather—and the days stretched to weeks, the weeks to months, and still he lay there, nursed by his mother and Gascoyne and Prior Edward, and now and again by Sir James Lee.

One day, a little before the good priest returned to St. Mary's Priory, as he sat by Myles' bedside, his hands folded and his sight turned inward, the young man suddenly said, "Tell me, father, it is always wrong for man to slay man?"

The good priest sat silent for so long a time that Myles began to think he had not heard the question. But by and by he answered, almost with a sigh, "It is a hard question, my son, but in truth it seems to me it is not always wrong."

"Sir," said Myles, "I have been in battle when men were slain, but never did I think about it as I have upon this matter. Did I sin in so slaying my father's enemy?"

"Nay," said Prior Edward, quietly, "ye did not sin. It was for others ye did fight, my son, and for others it is pardonable to do battle. Had it been your own quarrel, it might have been more hard to have answered you."

One day the Earl of Mackworth came to visit Myles. At that time the young knight was mending, and was sitting propped up with pillows wrapped in Sir James Lee's cloak, for the day was chilly. After a little talk, a pause of silence fell.

"My lord," said Myles suddenly, "do ye remember one part of a matter we spoke of when I first came from France?"

The Earl made no pretense of ignorance. "I remember," said he quietly, looking straight into the young man's thin white face.

"And have I yet won the right to ask for the Lady Alice de Mowbray to wife?" said Myles, the red rising faintly to his cheeks.

"Ye have won it," said the Earl, with a smile.

Myles' eyes shone, and his lips trembled with the pang of sudden joy and triumph, for he was still very weak. "My lord," said he presently, "perhaps ye came to see me on this very matter?"

The Earl smiled again without answering, and Myles knew that he had guessed right. He reached out one of his weak, pallid hands from beneath the cloak. The Earl of Mackworth took it with a firm pressure, then instantly dropping it, rose, as if ashamed of his emotion, stamped his feet, as though in pretense of being chilled, and then crossed the room to where the fire crackled brightly in the great stone fireplace.

Little else remains to be told. Only a few loose strands to tie, and the story is complete.

Though Lord Falworth was saved from death at the block, though his honor was cleansed from stain, he was still as poor and needy as ever. The King, in spite of all the pressure brought to bear upon him, refused to restore the estates of Falworth and Easterbridge—the latter of which had again reverted to the crown upon the death of the Earl of Alban without issue— on the grounds that they had been forfeited not because of the attaint of treason, but because of Lord Falworth's having refused to respond to the citation of the courts. So the business dragged

251

along for month after month, until in January the King died suddenly in the Jerusalem Chamber at Westminster. Then matters went smoothly enough, and Falworth and Mackworth swam upon the flood tide of fortune.

So Myles was married, for how else should the story end? And one day he brought his beautiful young wife home to Falworth Castle, which his father had given him for his own, and at the gateway he was met by Sir James Lee and by the newly knighted Sir Francis Gascoyne.

One day, soon after his homecoming, as he stood with his wife at an open window into which came blowing the pleasant May breeze, he suddenly said, "What did ye think of me when I first fell almost into your lap, like an apple from heaven?"

"I thought ye were a great, goodhearted boy, as I think ye are now," said she, twisting his strong, sinewy fingers in and out.

"If ye thought me so then, what a very fool I must have looked to you when I so clumsily besought you for your favor for my jousting at Devlen. Did I not so?"

"Ye did look to me the most noble, handsome young knight that ever did live. Ye did look to me Sir Galahad, without taint or stain."

Myles did not even smile in answer, but looked at his wife with such a look that she blushed a rosy red. Then, laughing, she slipped from his hold, and before he could catch her again was gone.

I am glad that he was to be rich and happy and honored and beloved after all his hard and noble fighting.